CHROME DOME DEATH

Rockson was suddenly confronted by a huge shape silhouetted against the raging fires in the camp. It wasn't human, that was certain. Its half-torn-away uniform revealed glistening chrome and steel parts. In a frightening metallic voice it uttered three words:

"You die here."

"Not today," Rock said emphatically. He opened up with his shot pistol, firing directly at the thing's chest. Bullets ricocheted off metal. It should have been blasted to bits, but it stood. Rock fired again, spraying the giant gleaming metal thing with the rest of his cartridges. Nothing. Then it smiled and began moving forward.

"Time to die, Rockson."

DOOMSDAY WARRIOR

#9 AMERICA'S ZERO HOUR

BY RYDER STACY

ZEBRA BOOKS
KENSINGTON PUBLISHING CORP.

ZEBRA BOOKS

are published by

Kensington Publishing Corp.
475 Park Avenue South
New York, NY 10016

First printing: November 1986

Printed in the United States of America

Chapter 1

Like the red mists of hell itself, the radioactivity from level eight drifted along the concrete corridor as if hoping for flesh to burn, cells to disintegrate. It rolled back and forth between the ice-cold cement walls in waves of purple, glowing like the phosphorescent death-creatures among coral reefs. These gaseous waves contained hot death for those mad enough to enter their domain.

Ted Rockson, his mismatched violet and aquamarine eyes watching from behind the leaded glass of his helmet for the slightest sign of impending collapse of the tunnel ahead, walked slowly forward leading a team of Freefighters. All wore the anti-rad suits of white, leaded asbestos and layers of plasteel.

The rad-suits made them appear to be a good foot taller than they actually were as they lumbered awkwardly through the narrow passageway. On their chests were small Geiger counters that chattered incessantly, screaming out warning. The going was agonizingly slow as falling rocks and twisted beams blocked their way like an obstacle course. Through the rectangular leaded glass of their faceplates the others nervously watched Rockson and Chen edge forward and carefully place small explosive charges in the maze of debris. Wires were attached to a detonator. Then the nine-man team rushed back down the corridor and around the bend.

This part of Century City had been sealed off, untouched, since the nuke attack by Killov's bomber's several months earlier. But now it had to be opened and restored. Some on the Century City Council, Intel Chief Rath for one, had pleaded to keep this section closed forever—an eternal tomb for those who lay mangled and crushed inside. But others, including Rockson, had vehemently opposed the concept.

"Century City lives," he had told the council at the debate. "No part of it should remain a tomb. We honor our dead more by carrying on what they worked all their lives for—a fully functioning city— than by letting them rot in darkness!" His faction had won. And now the dirty work had to be done.

Century City: born over 100 years earlier, in a rage of atomic fires. Originally it was just a highway tunnel that collapsed at both ends when nukes hit nearby, sealing hundreds of cars, trucks, and trailers in its blackness. Back then, on Interstate 70 winding out of Denver and into the mountains toward Utah, thousands of vehicles had been moving through the five-mile tunnel that bored through the heart of the mountain. The nukes that struck Colorado Springs, Longmont, and Fort Collins quaked the Rockies, and the tunnel entryways were buried in an ava-

lanche of rocks, sealing off the sea of humanity. It saved those trapped inside the eight-lane tunnel from the direct effects of the blasts, and from the rain of fallout which obscured the sun for weeks.

Those that survived, men and women and children from all the cross sections of American culture, divvied up the food and water from two tractor-trailers trapped inside that were filled to the brim with supermarket goods. Then they looked at one another and tried to figure out just what the hell to do. Days later they burrowed through the eastern entrance to the tunnel for air, which they cleansed through makeshift filtration systems. However, they soon understood the magnitude of what had happened: The first man to step out sighted Soviet airlifters dropping troops over Denver.

The Reds weren't content with wiping out half of America—they wanted to take it over as well.

Survival was the name of the game now—the highway-people cleaned themselves off again and went to work. The dreams, careers, loves, and hates that had meant everything to them just days before were now but dust blown into the stratosphere by nuclear devastation. They concentrated on constructing some kind of base, a headquarters to live in and from which they could strike out at the Russians.

Leaders emerged—men like Bonne and Ostrader who were determined to do more. They would build an underground city networking nearby mining tunnels and the tunnel of Interstate 70. They would set up lighting, ventilation, even hydroponics for the cultivation of their own food supply! The involuntary dwellers of this new subterranean world in-

7

cluded mavens in almost every field—scientists, doctors, chemists, mechanics. Most important, they were Americans. They were the people whose country had been born of guts and imagination and an eternal struggle for freedom. They swore they all would one day be free again—even if it took a hundred years. Hence, they named their subterranean home Century City.

Rockson set the detonator down and yelled through the helmet to the team. "Duck your heads. I've seen blast shrapnel come around corners." The men did so, and with a final check to make sure everyone was back, he pressed the detonation switch. There was a loud *whump* and a rolling echo. Then a choking cloud of dust nearly blotted out the beams of the lanterns mounted atop their helmets.

When the dust finally settled enough to see, they pressed forward into the smoky maelstrom, into the graveyard of their fellow Freefighters. They passed the first bodies—a child and a man huddled together. The man's back had been crushed from the fall of a beam. When the nuke had hit he had probably tried to shelter the small child half under him. The bodies were greenish with rot. Rockson gritted his teeth, pushing down a sickly feeling in his guts. In the other parts of the city all seemed almost back to normal. But here . . . The moldering corpses of the butcher Killov's handiwork paid mute testimony to the maniac's evil.

"Bastard," Chen muttered just behind Rockson as his eyes focused down on the little crushed face, its features melted together like a doll thrown in a vat of acid. "I think it's Cindy Adams," the Chinese fighter yelled through the helmet—the one disadvantage of the thick anti-rad suits and visors being that it was hard as hell to communicate through them—"and her father . . . he had been bringing her to my children's classes in self-defense. She would have been good, Rock, real good."

But there wasn't time to mourn—not when they saw the pile of bodies squeezed tightly together in the chamber. *They had been on an excursion—a dozen children and three adults—showing the youth of Century City the full extent of their subterranean haven. Then the bomb had hit.* The bodies rippled with a flickering radioactive incandescence.

"Looks like high-rad contam," said the stocky black cannonball of a man called Detroit Green.

"Too much radiation," Rock answered. "We've got to vent this tunnel—get the gases, the particles, outside. There should be an emergency exit just around this curve, according to the map."

"I've got the M87-K charges wired and ready, Rock," Detroit said, a basket of the high-explosive goodies tucked under his arm.

"Not too much, Detroit, we can only afford to make a small vent hole to the outside—get rid of some of this trapped radon gas. The bigger the blast, the more likely the damned red spy drones will see it—and we don't want to disrupt the blackout on Carson Mountain."

Indeed, Schecter's demand for a blackout despite the men swarming above doing nightly restoration, graveling over the exposed areas, may have been

9

unnecessary. The Reds were embroiled in a civil war with each other—KGB versus Red Army. In fact, they were probably too busy to attack the Freefighters' main base again. But Schecter's motion had passed, over Intel Chief Rath's objections. Rath was a thorn in the side of the unanimity that had existed before Killov's attack. Rock noticed that Rath opposed anything that he or Schecter wanted to do.

The Doomsday Warrior was still nursing a grudge against Rath for managing to squeak through a reduction in the men and materials for his attack on Fort Minsk. In the end it hadn't mattered that much—the KGB-held fort had fallen anyway—but it could have.

The charges were again set, and the *whummppp* of fresh mountain air poured in as the wreckage blocking the shaftway was blasted free. The rad reading began decreasing in intensity within minutes as the gases and high-rad dust was sucked out by the pressure differential.

The team began to vacuum the walls and floor of the tunnel with small hand-held vacuums. The loose dust and powdery mountain pumice had to be contained. Only then could the secondary teams come in, remove the bodies, and begin the more careful decontamination of the entire area.

At first the cleanup was relatively easy, as the main tunnel was wide enough for them to go around portions that had caved in, but when they reached the beginning of the smaller side tunnels the going got rougher. At last the debris from the collapsed walls virtually stopped their progress. Rockson pulled out the blueprints of the elaborate tunnel system. There were hundreds of passageways—many of them built when the original highway had been linked with mineshafts over a hundred years earlier. There were tunnels for ventilation, for electrical connection, to different sections of the two-mile-long structure. In addition, thirty three-foot-wide thermal heat shaftways had been dug out over the last century by the builders of the Freefighting city. They contained hot steam from volcanic sources.

"Here, men," Rockson said, his voice swallowed by the helmet which had a small speaker-slot near his mouth.

He pointed to an archway that had debris filling it nearly to the ceiling. "This is Q Section—the entrance hall to some of the newer weapons labs. If we can get this tunnel cleared up we will have done our job—for today." Schecter had warned Rock not to keep the team in the high-rad zones for more than five hours. After that he wasn't going to guarantee the protective capabilities of the suits.

Detroit came forward on Rockson's wave of the hand. "Should I set a charge?" the ebony-faced Freefighter asked, his bull shoulders apparent even in the cumbersome suit.

Rockson looked at the wall of broken concrete. "A small one. If there's no tunnel beyond this debris, if Q Section is completely collapsed, a large explosion could send all its rubble shooting out at us. Put one—right in the middle—between those two big rocks. Set the charge for two point five."

Detroit carefully placed the cylindrical charges in a space between the cement boulders, and they all retreated to what they thought was a sufficient

11

distance. Rockson's hand pressed down the detonator.

But something went wrong. The tunnel shook with a volcanic concussion making the men's very bones vibrate. A storm of granite and collapsing concrete roared down toward them tearing the supports out from the main tunnel's reinforced walls. They turned and began running, but instantly were being pounded by the crumbling roof of the tunnel.

The flashbeams of their helmet lights were cracked by the torrent of debris. As they stumbled ahead in the near-total darkness, their breathing filters became clogged and the air in the helmets grew gritty and suffocating. And still the roaring continued. Rockson felt rather than saw the presence of the others behind, heard their heavy breathing, their yells to one another to keep together. Then he heard a scream just behind him—one of the men had been downed, slammed to the cold rock floor. It sounded like Lyons's voice. Rockson wanted to stop and turn, but the safety of all of them depended on him leading them forward out of this mess. Before they got buried alive!

All around Rockson the walls suddenly caved in— a boiling avalanche of boulders and powder. He dove forward with a powerful kick and hit the dirt in the clear corridor ahead, rolling over several times. He came up in a half-crouch, fished his auxiliary flash from his belt, and looked back. The entire tunnel, a distance of about thirty feet behind, had been sealed in by the collapse. He was alone.

He rose, and walked slowly forward, not sure if

12

more of the ceiling was about to fall down and squeeze him into pulp. He came up to the wedge of rocks covered with a flowing curtain of dust and screamed out at the top of his lungs, "Anyone there? Chen? Detroit?"

Nothing. He yelled again. "Anyone there? God-damn you, answer me, you bastards. You *can't* be dead. You can't be." He smashed the light against the granite wall in fury and then cursed himself for being so stupid. But the thing flickered and then kept shining, apparently willing to give him another chance.

Suddenly he heard a far-off muffled sound and leapt against the mound of debris pressing his helmet to it, trying to hear. He couldn't be sure if it was the groaning of another foundation beam giving way or a human voice. Then he heard it clearly: "Rooocccckkksssooonnnn." It was his friend Archer, the bearish-sized Freefighter. He was alive.

"I'm here, Archer—are you okay?" He flashed his beam all along the dusty holes in the collapsed material. He saw a hand through one of the spaces. He crawled forward—there was just about enough room in the tangle of debris to do so—for about fifteen feet. He saw a powdery face sticking out of the crush of rock and dust. And somehow Archer had a dumb smile plastered across his white-bearded jaw.

Rockson pushed slowly on the oval-shaped boulder that was squarely atop the giant man's chest. After seconds, it rolled to the side, without dislodging the tunnel wall. Archer sucked in a huge gasp as he had barely been able to breathe and tried to rise in the confined space.

"Anyone else—did you see anyone else go down?" Rockson asked the four-hundred-pound-plus mountain man.

Archer nodded, and pointed to his side to a rabbit-hole of an opening. Rockson played his light on it. It was the small alcove that they had passed—just an access to a storage area—could the team be alive in there?

"Archer, are you hurt?" Can you help me?" Rock asked.

"Yesss. Meeee help," Archer growled. They moved some debris carefully and reached the small opening Archer had indicated.

Rockson had Archer hold his immense back against a partially collapsed main beam while he crawled forward to the hole, praying the bear of a man would be able to hold up that part of the tunnel—otherwise there'd be no escape. The Doomsday Warrior crawled forward barely able to fit through, found the narrow hallway beyond. He saw a shape in the light beam.

"Rock—Heavy," Archer groaned behind him. Rockson couldn't make out the shape down the jagged passageway, but it was roundish. He waited for the dust he had disturbed to settle before he was sure. It was a body, a human body in a rad-suit. The Doomsday Warrior's face blanched as he pulled the helmet off. The man's teeth popped out like broken marbles, the head cleanly severed from the crushed bloody torso of a body. Shit—he couldn't even tell who it was anymore. His heart began to sink down into his feet: they were dead. After all the Russian armies, the mutations, the acid storms . . . Chen,

Detroit, all of them, gone in the rubble of their own city, due to his own error.

Suddenly he saw a slit of illumination ahead, like a sword cutting through the stew of swirling dust.

"Anyone there?" he screamed. It could just be one of the headlamps dropped to the ground, with a crushed skull sitting in the helmet beneath it. "Anyone—anyone at all, can you hear me?" Rockson listened with his senses on full alert for the slightest confirmation of life. Then he heard it—indistinct at first, just a slight tapping sound. But regular—in patterns of threes. Someone was alive in there.

"Archer!" Rockson commanded, swinging around halfway inside the precarious tunnel. The ceiling shifted uneasily above him as if debating whether to fall and crush the puny flesh to an oozing slime. "You've got to hold, understand?—got to stay there."

"Arrrcher stay," the immense Freefighter said with a sigh of resignation. He looked up at the tons of weight he was barely able to keep aloft—his body pressed with all the might of his tree-size legs against the main upright timber at the very edge of the secondary tunnel. It squeaked and cracked with a most alarming volume. But he held.

Rockson turned forward again, gulped, and started crawling down the narrow passageway, the air gray with clouds of fine dust. He was able to move forward another fifteen feet, sliding around the beams that lay snapped, the timbers sliced jaggedly, their splinters reaching up trying to snag him. At last he could go no further, as he came face to face with a wall of collapsed granite and concrete. Rock put his

15

mouth up against the narrow crack along one side where he saw a shaft of light. He spit out the grit and yelled.

"Anyone alive? Anyone at all?"

"Rock! Rock? Is that you?" a voice came back from the other end, sounding as dim and muffled as if it was from the moon.

"Yeah, I hear you, thank God," Rockson yelled, letting his taut gut relax for the first time. He had been sure they had all died except Archer.

"It's Chen, Rock. Believe it or not, we're all here except Archer and Harrison. Bruises, blood. But everyone's alive."

"Listen pal, there's no time for talk!" Rock screamed back. "And there's no time for digging you out. This whole area looks like it's going to go anytime. And once it does, it's curtains for all of you. I remember that this passageway comes to a dead end about fifty feet behind you, with nothing but solid granite mountains for a full half-mile. We have to go out my way—and it's hell. There's ten or fifteen feet of heavy debris between me and you. I've got to do something—drastic."

"Go ahead, Rock, we're with you—whatever you decide," Chen shouted back. "Good luck."

"I'd hoped you'd say that," the Doomsday Warrior screamed, his lips pressed between the edges of cold stone. "Now get back—all of you. I've got two charges left on my belt. I'm going to wedge them about halfway down this wall here and try to blast the motherfucker open. Archer is playing Atlas beyond me. The moment the blast ends, run, you hear me?—run like wolves are on your ass, even if I'm . . . not around."

16

"Roger," Chen yelled. "We're heading to the back. Will rendezvous in about ten seconds. Hope I see you again."

"Me too," Rockson muttered as he pulled back from the space and took the cylindrical charges out. The thought of their deaths at his hands wasn't something he could let himself ponder. He pushed in with his arm, as far as he could, until the explosive packs were over a yard into the blockage. He shimmied backward until he was just shielded by a barrel-sized chunk of mountain that had fallen down, and pressed the detonation switch. The entire world around him shook as if he were in the grip of a vengeful God's hand and it was being squeezed tighter every second. The roar, the dust, the powerful vibrations of the passage floor, all disoriented Rock for a few seconds as he barely realized where he was. Then it stopped, the echoes rolling down the myriad passages and tunnels of the mountain and a flood of thick dust pouring toward him. And in the midst of it—a running shape, and then another.

"Should have known you'd be asleep on the job," Chen said as he rushed to Rockson almost slamming into him in the near darkness. Chen helped Rock stand and move out.

The rad-suit-clad survivors ran in half-crouches down the smoky passage. "Link hands," Rock shouted. They did; it was the blind leading the blind in the impenetrable smoke. After thirty feet, the beam of the lamp somehow lit enough of a line of sight to just avoid the spearlike beams and twisted spears of metal that probed out from everywhere. Chen was holding Rock's hand, and Detroit behind him his, so that all the way down the line, they were connected

17

like a rock-climbing team. It was not the time to get left behind.

Rock saw Archer ahead, straining with every ounce of his incredible strength to keep the tunnel entrance from collapsing down around them. When he reached him, Rockson squeezed alongside him and pushed with his back as well, as the line of men rushed past them into the more-open tunnel ahead. There was no time left. The charges had been the last straw. Though they pushed with their combined power, the entire frame was going—the support beam shrieking out a high-pitched sound as its hard wooden guts snapped in two. Archer suddenly jumped free from the side and threw his arms under the crossbeam as if trying to take the entire weight of the mountain. Titans had done less in ancient days of myth, than Archer did now. But he was just a man. And Rockson knew the loyal fool would stay there forever to save the rest of them.

"I'm not leaving till you come," he yelled out as he readied himself to move. "On the count of three, we both let go and get the hell out of here. Okay, you understand?"

"Uu-nnd'rrstan," the giant Freefighter managed to croak out through lips drained of blood.

"One, two—three!" Rockson screamed, and they both shot away from the archway and toward the tunnel where the rest of the team was waiting for them. The arch gave way the moment they pulled free and came down toward them even as they moved away. The dust and the falling rocks and chunks seemed to almost reach out for the two fleeing humans as if not wanting them to get away. They both tore ass into the wider tunnel, the beams of the ceiling cracking just behind them, one after another, as if following them down the passage.

"Move, move," Rock screamed at the stalled line, and Chen in the lead took off. They say sometimes the main part of valor is to know when to run, to run with every bit of strength and heart you have. And now was such a time. Eight of the toughest fighters in America tore down the half-blocked passages without a glance back. Ran as the lowest level of Century City collapsed all around them. Ran even as the noise at last receded behind them, and the cave-in came to a stop. At last they reached the ramp to the higher level and slowed down, collapsing in a gasping heap on the floor. They lay there long minutes, each man praying to his own private God, in thanks for another reprieve in the eternal chess game of death. They doffed their helmets. Rockson caught Archer looking at him with a pleased expression in his grime-coated eyes.

"You did well, pal," the Doomsday Warrior said as he rose to his feet. "I'm recommending you for the city's highest decoration."

Archer growled, "Meee—goood!"

Once back in the living levels of Century City, the men went through the decontamination procedure to ensure that no radioactive material was allowed to come into the city. They came to a room filled with telephone-booth-sized chambers and disrobed, putting the high-rad suits in special lead deposit boxes.

Rock entered the enclosed glass chamber. The door

19

closed with a slam, followed by a sudden rush of air as the atmosphere Rock carried with him from the radioactive area lifted and was replaced by Century City's tri-filtered air.

"Remove all rings," a pleasant female voice purred from a hidden speaker.

"I've done it already," Rock answered in a tired voice, having gone through the same routine countless times.

"That's fine," the voice replied. "Stage One will now begin." A soft chime followed and then violet lights spilled over the floor and ceiling. From inset sprinklers, a shower of water cascaded down on Rockson, cleansing him with a mixture of suds and disinfectants. The water, shot down under high pressure, gave his body a rather pleasant, tingling sensation. After twenty seconds he was rinsed off with pure water.

"Stage Two," the voice intoned as dazzling violet beams danced over his body, creating hypnotic strobes of phosphorescent color. He sealed his eyes shut, viewing the light show through his lids. All personnel were equipped with dark glasses for the procedure, but Rockson knew that his mutant eyes could withstand the energy spectrum. His retinas were not the same as those of *Homo sapiens*. Rockson could look directly into the burning face of the sun without harming them.

"Stage Three." A low humming sound built up beneath his feet, growing in intensity until it filled the chamber with a physical presence. Rockson could feel the million-times-a-second vibration caused by the sound waves hold his body in a blurring grip. The sonic waves were literally shaking loose any bits of radioactive particles that were trying to take root in the Freefighter's skin. At last it was over, and the door opened again with a flash.

"Thank you," the voice said softly.

"Yeah, thanks, lady," Rock answered the speaker as he stepped out. "I hope it was as good for you as it always is for me." He put on the set of carefully folded coveralls that had been automatically deposited on a table next to the chamber. The lightweight white cotton one-piece outfit felt good, cool against his skin, after the anti-rad suit's stifling coarseness.

Chapter 2

As he walked through the wide central square of the underground city, Rockson picked Rath and Shannon out of the crowd of milling workers and technicians who were observing a "street performer's" magic act. Rath, the intel chief for the City, was a slow, stooped, gray-headed man. Still, he was a commanding figure somehow, with his hawklike nose and the heavy eyebrows, under which rested the deep gray eyes of a man of suspicious nature and high intelligence. Shannon, his assistant, was a well-endowed, strawberry-blond woman of about thirty years of age. She counterbalanced the dour, moody Rath with a bright-eyed efficiency and optimism. Rockson knew them both very well. Rock was about to pass them by, as he had things to do, but Rath's keen eyes caught him, and the intel chief called him over with a brisk wave. Rock frowned. When Rath wanted to speak to you, it was hardly ever anything you wanted to hear. But it usually was important.

"What's up, Rath? How are you, Shannon?" Rock

took in her red skin-tight one-piece. "New outfit?" he asked.

"Rockson," Rath sneered, "I heard about your near disaster in the tunnel. I'd like to discuss with you soon—in private—your tendency to foolhardy reckless adventure for the sake of adventure. Not just today, but at Fort Minsk—on many occasions. You seem to forget your rank, your responsibilities, your—"

"This doesn't sound very private," Rockson cut him off. "So how about tomorrow, at lunch, in your office? I'll bring the sandwiches. That all?" Rock turned on his heels.

Rath shouted after him as he left, "You be there tomorrow at noon. You hear? Be there. No man's bigger than the whole. You've got to obey the rules."

Shannon seemed torn for a minute between her boss and Rockson, but then took after the Doomsday Warrior, catching up to him out of sight of Rath. "Please don't be mad at me for Rath's bad mood—what he said . . ."

Rockson stopped in mid-stride and said, "I can't see how you can work with the man. He's nasty, and gets nastier every day—and besides that, he's opposed to and continues to oppose almost every idea I have for waging the war against Killov and Vassily."

"He works so hard . . ." Shannon said softly. "The responsibilities of his job are immense. That's why he is the way he is. Give him the benefit of the doubt. You know how invaluable his network of spies and saboteurs in the Russian fortress cities are. He is really a very sensitive, compassionate man. That's his problem. He hides the fact that his heart hurts every time he finds out that one of his operatives is caught and tortured to death. Rath is responsible for us knowing when Zhabnov so much as twitches, or where Killov is slinking around. And he feels the weight of all of it—of the whole damned war against the Reds—on *his* shoulders."

Rockson softened to her. "You're right. Things have been bad—one disaster after another. The strain must be too much for him. God knows how any of us stay sane in all of this. I'll cool out, Shannon, I promise. And you—give him less coffee, or else put tranquilizers in his cup, okay?"

Shannon agreed with a laugh and Rock headed on to one of the spacious cafeterias, the Starlight, where he pressed buttons for a tray full of simple but nourishing food—rabbit stew, soybean cheese, and two big slabs of whole-grain bread. But he had barely made it off to a secluded corner table and lifted a steaming spoonful to his mouth when a finger tapped insistently at his shoulder. He smelled jasmine perfume. "Okay, Rona, you seem to want to tell me something . . ."

Rona Wallender, all red-haired, stacked five feet ten inches of her leaned over the table. He turned to see that her bright green eyes were watery. "Oh, Rock, when I heard that there had been a collapse in the tunnel you were working in, I—" She finished the sentence by lightly kissing him on the cheek. She stared into his intense eyes, the eyes that she knew had seen so much pain and suffering. She quivered with emotion. "I told myself, and God, that if you came out of the tunnel all right, I would stop this silly staying away from you, stop it and tell you I love you. I don't care if you love Kim too. As long as you want me, I'll be yours."

"Rona," Rock said, pecking her on the cheek, "I'm glad. I do love you. I'll always love you. What I haven't liked is your trying to be the only woman in my life. It—can't be—now. You understand—since I met Kim . . ."

Rona touched his brawny tanned arm on the table, squeezing it hard. "I want to come to your room tonight—at nine. Is that okay?"

Rockson put his hand over hers. "Yes."

She grew suddenly bright and smiling. "But don't tell Kim I gave in. We promised each other that neither of us would sleep with you until you made up your mind which one you wanted as a lover."

"Mum's the word," Rock grinned, knowing he was heading for trouble again.

Rona unbuttoned her blouse. Her full breasts and their cream-white nipples seemed to swell like ripe fruit waiting to be plucked. Flushed with desire, she boldly put her long hands out and tore at his pants until they fell to the floor in a heap. She slowly got down on her knees and kissed his manhood, making it stand up, eager, ready, steel-hard. Moans of pleasure came softly through her lips as her tongue slid down the swollen shaft. Rock held Rona's head, his fingers ran through her fiery locks.

Her lips moved up and down the long stiff rod, trying to fit its entire length in her throat. Rock reached down and squeezed her firm, full breasts, and then, putting his arms around her, he lifted her up to him as if the slender woman were as light as a feather. He grabbed her behind each of her tan thighs and pulled her up onto him. She guided the long spear of flesh into her, slowly. Rona groaned, her eyes closing, her head dropping back as the stiff organ penetrated her to the core. Her long legs wrapped around his waist, then locked together. He began pumping, slowly at first, and as their passions grew, faster, until he was a jackhammer inside her, her triangle of red hair dripping with the juices of passion. Rock gripped her even closer to him, moving her legs apart, pushing into the deepest recesses of her supple body, taking her to the peak of pleasure.

Grinding against him, crushing her breasts against his muscled chest, Rona went into her special kind of mutant frenzy, as waves of sensation steamed up from her core. Her head thrashed back and forth, her eyes closed as the softest of catlike noises escaped from her pink lips. Rockson hadn't made love to Rona for months. Yet their bodies *followed* each other's slightest nuance. Perfect. His eyes shut, he felt his life-giving fluid rise up and shoot through his male organ, pumping into her with powerful thrusts. As he came in a violent eruption, her entire form went rigid and then jerked wildly against him. The woman seemed to be trying to push him all into her—completely. For a moment, they merged into one being, joined together in the mindless bliss as old as time itself. Then they lay down spent, exhausted, fulfilled.

An hour after Rona left, there was a gentle knock

on Rock's door. He thought perhaps she was back and went to the door nude, opening it a crack. There, clad in a gold semitransparent halter and an equally thin and clinging miniskirt, was Kim. She lifted her sky-blue eyes at Rock and whispered to the man towering over her five foot two inch ultra-feminine form, "Can I come in?"

Rockson gulped, let her in. Kim moved gingerly, as the only illumination in the room was from the glow of the twisted elk horns he had on his dresser, a souvenir of one of his treks into the unknown lands. Its dull glow didn't disturb sleep and was enough to move around the room in.

"Rock," she said softly, grabbing him around his muscular waist, "Don't turn on the lights—there is enough—for making love." Rockson had lived long enough in this world to know that sometimes one had to just go with the flow. Having both women he was in love with in Century City at the same time had its problems, but it also had its pleasures. Double pleasures.

She undid a hidden clasp and her halter slipped down and fell on the floor, revealing her creamy large breasts and upturned nipples. Another quick movement and the gold miniskirt likewise dropped to the floor displaying Kim's wispy platinum hair in the vee of her legs. The area caught the red glow of the horn. "Please don't tell Rona I broke our agreement. But I *had* to come. I had to—feel you. You're not mad, are you?"

"No," Rockson smiled weakly. "Not at all."

"I can't stay more than an hour—Rona is so jealous that she sometimes checks on my room to make sure I'm there and living up to our agreement to not sleep with you until you decide which one of us—" She didn't finish her run-on sentence because Rockson had lifted her up and carried her effortlessly to the bed. "No, I won't tell"—he pressed his lips to hers—"if you won't."

Chapter 3

Rock had no idea what time it was, but he awoke to an insistent knocking on his door. Kim was gone—and the sheets were thick with sweat and the sweet, animal smell of sex. Rock stumbled to the door grabbing a towel which he wrapped around him. He opened it. One of the graveyard-shift communications techs was standing there, his hand raised up with a typewritten paper in it.

"Message, sir," the tech said, snapping to attention at being face to face with Ted Rockson—among other things, Century City's ranking military officer. "We picked this up just twenty minutes ago on one of our standard Russian radio interceptions. It was for your attention, sir. I hope I didn't disturb you!"

"No, you did the right thing, thanks." Rock took the message and held it up beneath the low light of the ceiling lamps along the hall . . .

Ted Rockson: In return for Freefighter help in defeating Colonel Killov at Fort Minsk and for helping to clear other KGB-held areas of the United Soviet States of America, I am going through with my promise to remove all nuclear weapons from the American continent. I know you have sufficient intelligence sources to verify the fact that they will be hauled out by airlifter and boat over the next 2 weeks. But I must warn you, Killov has seized 5 truck-mounted cruise missiles from an arsenal in Idaho Sector. He has headed north. We lost track of him in Canada. Make contact with me in order to coordinate our efforts to neutralize Killov and these weapons. End of message.

"Don't break radio silence," Rockson ordered the tech, "I'll take care of this. It's a military matter. Confidential."

"Sir," the man snapped, and tore off back to his post.

Schecter fairly ran down the corridor, a most peculiar jerking, leaning sort of run for an old man. But he didn't have regular legs. They had been half-blown-off by a blast of Nazi fire three months ago. But the injury had just propelled Schecter's brilliance in a new direction—servomechanical limbs for paraplegics. He invented his own legs—a fantastic breakthrough in technology that had spelled hope to many Freefighters crippled by the damned endless war with the Sov occupation forces.

Rockson turned the corner and saw Schecter barreling toward him yelling "Out of the way, out of the way" like a schoolboy on a skateboard. They entered the conference room together.

Rath was already seated, Shannon at his side. He looked up from his papers, his eyes magnified behind his strong pince-nez reading glasses, the nostrils in his large nose flared, and he frowned as a way of greeting. Rockson didn't bother to say hello, instead, nodding to Shannon when she looked up, he slid a chair out for Dr. Schecter who seemed to be having a bit of difficulty with the maneuver.

"Don't help me," Schecter insisted, "Just a little adjustment problem. I've solved walking and running—but the damned servomechanism doesn't want to shuffle, which is what you have to do with your feet to pull your own chair out." With those words Schecter opened his shirt and revealed a control panel on his belt buckle with more buttons on it than a pocket calculator. He began pressing in instructions with his fingers, and his legs kind of vibrated his feet back. He put the chair in, slid it out from the table again. Then his legs sort of hummed over to the side, shuffled against the chair, and his knees bent, slowly and perfectly lowering him into the seat. Then a dozen shuffling movements of his electrofeet slid the chair forward to the table.

Dr. Schecter smiled broadly, "See?"

"Can we *begin?*" Rath said. "Although you didn't notify me, Rockson, I was told of your *secret* message from Vassily. That's what I want to discuss at this meeting." Rockson found the remark rather offensive, but let it go.

"Heck," said Schecter, looking pleased. "The legs will remember those instructions now whenever I

33

want to sit at a table like this. The memory chips—"

"The meeting, the *meeting!*" Rath half-snarled. He looked back at Rockson. "It would certainly appear from the contents of this message that Vassily expects you to agree to an alliance with his forces versus Killov. Only the council can vote on such a thing. It's written in our city's very Constitution. Are you holding yourself above the politics of the citizens of this greatest and freest of America's hidden cities?"

"It is a military matter, Rath—you know that. We might have to coordinate with the Red Army to fight the worse enemy—Killov and his KGB. That battle is not yet over. Killov has escaped."

Rath was unimpressed. "Rockson, you call it a military matter, but I call it a political move. You cannot act without a debate in the council, and I will oppose you tooth and nail."

Rockson replied, "There was a vote from the council. Rath, before I left for Fort Minsk I was given the authority, in advance, to carry out any course of action I chose to make, to win the damned battle against Killov. The council agreed with me that it was a military matter. We've already carried out our part. Vassily is now going to carry out his. All the nuclear weapons in America are to be taken away. It's a tremendous victory."

"All the nukes, except five," Rath said icily. "It's all a trick—that's what I think. A plot between Premier Vassily and Colonel Killov to get us. Somehow, someway—to get us, and destroy us."

Rockson looked hard at Rath. The man had been invaluable, if a bit gloomy, until the past few months. Now he seemed to have gone off his rocker.

Rockson had no more time for the man's personal problems. No one had time anymore for bullshit. He said as much.

Rath grabbed the letter and put on his pince-nez reading glasses. He read it and tossed it back on the table. "Democracy is being usurped by the military, just as I said—Rockson tried to hush this up. I know the intent behind it."

"I hardly think that's the case," Dr. Schecter said as he lit up his pipe. He had taken to smoking again lately. "I've seen Rockson work with the council. He has great respect for them and for the source of their power—the people. As I remember, Rock was given authority at the military convention of all the Freefighting cities to make his own determination about any link-up with the Red Army. Such a council, according to *our* bylaws, would supersede any Century City council."

"Technically correct," Rath said, looking displeased. "But that convention body is dissolved. Our city's council must be the source of all decisions again."

Rockson sat down again, exhaled some breath, and said, "Regardless of the 'technicalities,' a decision has to be made *now*. I propose to contact Vassily from a safe location some distance away from Century City. Rath, how about it?—for the sake of the freedom you cherish . . ."

Shannon put her hand on Rath's arm as he was about to respond hastily. "Dr. Rath," she said, "for me. Please, this once, go along with Rockson."

The old man seemed visibly moved by her plea. After a moment, he exhaled a breath and nodded.

Dr. Schecter said, "Now that it's settled . . . Rockson, is the relay station a hundred miles north of here—the one you previously contacted Vassily from—still in operation?"

"I don't know. We ripped it up a bit." Rock raised an eyebrow. "If Intel Division could supply us that information . . ."

Rath took a small looseleaf notebook from his suit jacket, and started thumbing through it. Rock had seen the book before. It was Rath's little dictionary containing constantly updated information from spies, mountainmen, and Russian radio broadcasts deciphered from their complex codes. The intel chief looked up when he found what he was looking for. "It's out of operation. The Reds moved everything out. But there is a radio base about fifty miles further on." He smiled triumphantly. "At least you see that I am up on my job, even if you and I don't always have smooth sailing."

"Sure," Rock said, trying to dredge up a smile. "Well, that's still on the way to Idaho, where the missiles were stolen from. Perhaps we could pick up the trail there. Where exactly is it?"

"Coordinates K-23 on our Soviet field map," Rath said dryly.

"Yes, K-23. If I radio Vassily from there, it would save time, and not give away Century City. Time is of the essence. I know Killov—he will not hesitate to use those weapons as soon as he can. And I think the Rockies are going to be their target. There'll be nothing left."

"Killov's position makes him doubly desperate," Shannon added. "He has lost everything. Just a few supporters among KGB sympathizing officers in Siberia and the men that helped him steal the cruise missiles remain of all his huge KGB force."

"Let's get cracking," said the Doomsday Warrior. "I have a hunch—call it mutant's premonition—that Killov is heading way into the north. Perhaps he wants to be in range of Vassily as well as us. We have quite a job ahead of us. I'm glad we're at it *united.*"

Working as a team, Shannon, Rath, Schecter, and Rockson took out the maps and discussed the route to the K-23 radio station and beyond. The Doomsday Warrior's mood was infinitely better than just moments before. Americans, working together for the common goal, Rockson knew, had been the strongest force for freedom in history. It was only when they were divided, discordant, that they were ever beaten.

Rockson went to his room and meditated. It always helped in tough decisions. His mind cleared, he took pencil and pad up and started the list of men he would need.

Rockson wanted to bring the smallest force possible with him, knowing that a large team couldn't hope to catch up to Killov. A small, highly trained, tough group, men who could endure bitter cold and possibly long periods without shelter or food. Men who would be psychologically as well as physically fit for the rigors ahead. Men, in other words, ready to die.

Of course *Detroit Green*, the black Freefighter with the best grenade-throwing arm in the city. *Archer,* with his crossbow and myriad types of arrows, for an arrow could do what a bullet could—with a whisper. *Chen*, the martial arts master. The Chinese man with pencil-thin drooping moustache could move silently as a cat, could take out ten men in a flash. *McCaughlin*, with his great strength, nearly as great as Archer's. He tended to slow things slightly, but he had a knack for keeping up morale that more than made up for it. That would be critical. Besides, McCaughlin could make a palatable meal out of anything, from snake tails to thorn bushes.

But he needed more. Rock expected to go on from K-23, to follow Killov to the North Pole itself if that was where he was heading. He went down to the computer room which had been one of the first sections repaired after the near destruction of Century City. Five of the ten computer terminals in the far end of the room, filled with banks of futuristic machines and blinking lights, were fully repaired. Rockson went to the console he preferred to use—the last one over by the wall—and accessed into the central files with his personal I.D. number and code, "Badger."

He programmed in the qualities he was looking for—physical strength, experience in cold terrains, fighting ability. And special qualifications: He needed a linguist, to deal with whatever groups inhabited the area—and someone who knew how the hell to defuse an atomic missile, if they ever found them. The computer screen lit up with the names:

PEDERSEN, NEIL. Linguistics expert, first rank. Physical rating 9.5. Psych index 9. Rockson knew the young, nearly bald, stocky man. High intelligence, endurance, plus he got along well with Chen, who was one of his few buddies. Pedersen had translated seven Post-Nuke-war microlanguages—and had written a treatise on them.

FARRELL, TIMOTHY. Tim was a lanky, tall blond man, and, Rock knew, a favorite of the young ladies of Century City. He was also a marksman, trained in veterinary medicine, having studied the animal sciences—plus he was always begging Rockson to take him on a mission. He was about to get his wish now—in frozen spades! Farrell, though, according to the file displayed on the screen, had one drawback. He and Detroit had had a fight once, over some stupid remarks passed in a drinking party one New Year's Eve. But he knew Detroit was cooled-out enough to handle it.

ROBINSON, MICHAEL, AKA "CHET." The man was an anthropologist, an authority on North American tribes, and on an expedition like this he would be invaluable. Rockson, in his many forays out into the cruel Post-Nuke America, had found that it was peopled by often incomprehensible forms of society, each with their own customs and ways of surviving. And the misinterpretation of even one of their customs could mean death. Robinson was a feisty, red-bearded, salt-of-the-earth type. And the file said he was quite a mountaineer. The man was a good ten years older than any of the others—but he had recently been checked out as being in perfect health, Rock saw as the man's medical chart rolled into view. He'd do.

The last name the computer came up with was Reston. Reston would have been great, they had worked together before. The problem was, he had accumulated too much radiation exposure in the last mission. The man was a fighter, the best. But the invisible enemy that stalked the land—the radioactive particles of sand, the deadly pockets of radioactive gases that periodically were released from the upper atmosphere—they had made the man a near invalid, his immune system in shatters, always coughing, gums bleeding. Someone should have put his file in the Inactive Section. Rockson did it himself, feeling like a heel, but knowing the man would be dead within weeks if he took any more outside exposure. His fighting days were over.

Rockson called the entire team together in the conference room on C level and explained the mission. He told them that they were all volunteers. They could decline. None did so.

"Chen, I assign you and McCaughlin—you both seem to have a handle on the supply aspect of our plan—to quartermaster for us," Rockson said. "I want a detailed list of what we need sent to the quartermaster's office on D-3 level, and a duplicate for me."

"I had to open my big mouth," said big McCaughlin. "I hate lists and paperwork."

"The job's not complete until the paperwork is done," laughed Detroit, his smile beaming. He was glad to be going out again.

"And you, Detroit, I want you to make sure we have all the medical supplies we need. Work it out with Doc Elston—I hear you're quite friendly with her since she reattached your right arm in microsurgery a few months back."

Detroit's smile vanished. "And, pray tell, what might you be doing while we all work?"

Rock said, "There's plenty for me to do to get ready. I don't like the idea of using the 'brids as transportation. I want to check down in Veterinary Section, see if any back-bred dogs can be brought along. They're intelligent animals; I'd like to have some dog sleds made up if there are any suitable dogs down there. Some of Dr. Schecter's boys might be able to modify some carts, weld on skids. It's winter out there . . ."

Detroit said, "Rock I don't know how to tell you this—but the dogs are all dead. That section of the city collapsed, killing them all, when Century City was bombed."

"Shit," Rock uttered, "I had high hopes for the breeding program. Then it has to be horses. We can't take half-track vehicles, we'd run out of fuel—but, the 'brids can eat the winter vegetation as long as there is any—even evergreen boughs, if they're mashed up right. I've got to get maps microstated for the mission. As I told you, I don't know where we'll wind up, so we're taking along maps for every piece of land north of here."

Rockson assigned tasks to all the men—getting the 'brids, the weaponry from the arsenal, and so on. He went down to the map room. He was appalled that many areas of Canada had no current maps. He was given maps that hadn't been updated in a hundred years.

Rockson allowed some time for the men to say

good-bye to their loved ones. Then they met for final check-out at the clothing supply room. "Men, each of you take your size parkas. Sorry, only one color—white. For camouflage. The jackets are reversible, though. If we want to keep track of each other, we wear the red side out. Make sure you have everything. Once we get going, there's no stopping for winter long johns." That brought a laugh.

They loaded up the six pack-'brids with all the equipment of every variety that Century City had gathered in a hundred years: sweaters, insulated down parkas, Arctic boots, snow-blindness goggles—even a few harpoons for ice fishing. They staggered away under the overstuffed packs on their backs and in their arms, out to the waiting hybrids at the wide exit ramp.

It was five-thirty A.M. They hadn't slept that night, and yet each man was eager and alert. Rock had each man double-check his weapons. Each had a Liberator rifle, twenty banana-clips for it; a .12-gauge shotpistol and a dozen snap-clips; and two knives—one for throwing, another for hand-to-hand combat. In addition, Chen had his belt of star knives, some explosive-tipped. Detroit carried twin bandoliers of grenades—fifteen in all. Some were incendiaries. Archer wore a quiver of arrows—some highly specialized killers—over his shoulder, and had a crossbow tied to his huge saddle. Rock had the standard equipment—rifle, shotpistol, two knives. But his rifle was special. It was a laser-targetscoped beauty with an electro-engraving of Daniel Boone's likeness on the stock.

Chapter 4

At the first light of dawn, Rockson and his men mounted up in the open mouth of the northwest exit of the underground bastion. One by one they rode out into the purple sunrise. As the stars winked out like dying lightbulbs and the sun rose from its nightbed throwing its red cape off onto the snows of the Colorado peaks, the team descended into the wood valley. By the time they traversed the vast woodlands, Rock knew, it would be night again. The days of November were short, even at this latitude. He shuddered to think of the far north in the winter. In just a few weeks there would be no daylight at all where they just might wind up—at the Arctic Circle. *Black days.*

Rockson rode Snorter, a hybrid he had used as a mount for many years now. The creature was immensely strong and heavily pelted—the result of generations of breeding of wild mustangs affected by radiation exposure. Like Rockson, the horse was a mutation, *Mutaneous equinus,* better equipped for the Post-Nuke world than any horse that had ever lived.

The 'brids like Snorter and the other mounts that Rockson's men rode truly lived only when they ran. Their massive sinewy legs churned away like steam engines, as their mouths, gaping wide, sucked in oxygen to fuel their bodies. The attack team rode along in perfect unison at full gallop, each man leaning far ahead around the neck of his 'brid to cut down the wind. Even the Doomsday Warrior had a smile on his face as they raced across the purplish-lit land.

The winter had been slow in starting, fall drifting along apparently endlessly, the gift of warm desert winds coming up from Arizona. The aspens were masses of yellow that fell like confetti in the sudden gusts of wind, the fresh air so warm that you had to leave your flak jacket across the back of your saddle and you were never sweaty in your tee shirt. But then the wind shifted. The temperature dropped fifty degrees in fifteen minutes. Rock's 'brid whinnied in displeasure as the warm breezes became sprinkles of snow thrown by the wind as if some huge fist had pitched the flakes directly into the 'brid's face. The young birch trees bent over, their leaves falling in storms of color—red, orange, yellow. Men that just moments before had been in their tee shirts now had their winter parkas zipped up tight and their heads down. The snow didn't last, mostly it was wind and a few flurries, but a light frost fell on the dark green grass, a silent blanket of white, quickly covering it. They rode on, thinking private thoughts . . .

"Moose! Moose!" a voice suddenly bellowed out, shattering the momentary serenity. Rock turned in his saddle to see Archer, high on his steed. His face was flushed with excitement as he gestured wildly with his mitt-sized hands.

Rock directed his 'brid over to the hyperactive mountainman. Snorter stopped in his tracks when he saw the mounds of moose droppings steaming on the cold snow, and started sniffing at the big holes the moose had kicked out of the moss.

"Moose season, huh?" Rock said.

Archer merely grunted, flashing a broken-toothed smile. "Me hunt?" He pointed off at the trail of hoofprints that headed toward a hillock of pine trees.

"Easy there, pal, no," Rockson said. "If we see one on the way, okay, we'll take a shot at it and you'll have your mooseburgers—but we're not on a hunting trip. Not today. Sorry."

Archer's face—what you could see of it beyond the black, overgrown, tangled beard—was crestfallen. But he nodded assent. Rockson was the one man he obeyed.

Rockson got the party moving again, taking the lead. Moose. The species had been almost wiped out by the war. But in the past decade the Freefighters had run across the majestic horned beasts numerous times. Once he had seen a herd of nearly a hundred grazing out in the grassy plains. Like most twenty-first-century animals, they had mutated from the radiation. Superficially they looked pretty much like the moose of old—but of course they weren't. He knew the moose were now largely nocturnal. Their big yellow eyes were slit like a cat's, enabling them to gallop at top speed through the darkest forest and never bang into a tree. The slit-eyed moose were a hell of a lot meaner and harder to kill than those of old—but they tasted wonderful.

Chapter 5

They had proceeded another ten miles when Archer shouted again. They turned and saw a magnificent moose on a hillock. Archer's face broke into a wide, idiotic grin as he reached for his crossbow. The creature, with horns big enough for a man to sit in, was approaching them with a quizzical expression on its face. Suddenly there was a *whooosh* of a rocket as a white-and-red trail of fire shot from a copse of trees. The moose barely had time to look up, startled, when the missile hit it, blowing it into a million stew-size pieces.

"Russians," Rock yelled, knowing that no American would do such a thing—waste an animal like that for fun.

They shot for cover as several Reds came driving out of the woods, singing and drinking, unaware of the Freefighters' presence. They had hit a moose with one of a rack of rockets on the back of a flat-top truck. There were five more men on cycles and about twenty troopers in armored half-tracks—KGB Blackshirts.

But these were sloppier than he had ever seen. A few had vodka bottles in their hands or in their mouths. Usually KGB were rigid as steel—like their master of murder, Killov. They would pay for their carelessness.

"When I give the signal, waste them. Grenades ready—frags and phosphorus, okay, Detroit?"

"Star knives?" asked Chen.

"For the wheels," Rock said. "That ought to at least cripple a bunch of them, then use full auto fire, deployment method B." The Reds were making such noise partying that they neither heard nor saw Freefighters as they fanned out on the ridge overlooking the grisly scene of casual slaughter below. The KGBers were too busy laughing and grabbing pieces of moose—paws, parts of horn—for souvenirs to take back to mother Russia.

"Look, Nivski," the leader smiled, a major by his insignia, "I will mount this eight-prong horn over my fireplace in Murmansk."

The lieutenant, a tall scraggly blond man with a half-empty bottle glued to his lips was evidently on unusually comradely terms with the major, for he said, "They will never let you come back to Murmansk. You have grown too used to lax discipline now that Killov is gone. None of us will ever go back. Let us drink and hunt and rape. Use this land for some fun before the rads or the Red Army get us."

"You are right, comrade," said the major, poking the lieutenant in a drunken manner on his chest. "And just for being right, you can have the other horn."

"The damaged one? Thanks, thief. You keep the good one and give me the damaged one!"

The KGB ranks gathered around the drunken officers and sent out gales of raucous laughter as they weaved alcoholic dances around the fragmented creature. They were at the peak of humor when the Freefighters shot forward from their hiding places among the boulders firing their Liberator rifles on full automatic. Many of the Reds choked on their own blood before they even stopped laughing. The others dove for cover amongst the rocks and bushes around them. Their well-oiled Kalashnikovs began to speak their own brutal tongue, flames leaping barrels, searching for flesh. Rock, as he rolled for cover, was grazed by a lucky shot. He winced in pain as the slug tore through his arm. Chen saw Rock get pinned down, and since he was on the opposite flank of the shooter saw a chance to catch the man by surprise. He ran forward with a star knife in each hand until he was within twenty feet of the KGB'er. Just as the Red turned with his rifle, Chen unleashed his weapons. They spun through the air one after the other like homing pigeons of death. The first hit the man square in the throat, slicing in through the Adam's apple and jugular, spraying out blood. The second hit his chest and slid in between the ribs, slicing into the right lung which oozed air like a popped balloon.

Gagging on his own blood, the Blackshirt spun on his heels and pitched forward into the grass. His eyes rolled up like dull marbles.

Digging two more of the six-pointed star knives out of his belt, the martial arts master rolled under some Communist fire and managed to scramble to the cover of a fallen log. Bullets chipped away at the rotted wood, threatening to bury themselves in his flesh, but he lay flat as a pancake.

It's my turn now, thought Rock. He rushed out from his cover and blasted away with his shotpistol, at the group of Reds who were pouring fire down on the Chinese Freefighter. One KGBer got it in the head and leapt to his feet in a half-mad jerk, blood spitting from his mouth. He seemed to be staring at the hole between his eyebrows as he collapsed in a heap, half over his nearest comrade. This knocked the rifle from his friend's shoulder, and before he could regain it Rock was on him. His hunting knife flashed and dug deep in the man's throat.

The rest of the Reds—two huddled groups of five men each—lay behind rocks halfway up the opposite hill. They fired wildly at everything they saw or heard. And they heard a lot of rocks and pebbles that Chen and Rockson began throwing about the killing field. Dead stumps and small boulders were chipped by frenzied fire from the Kalashnikovs as they spent a lot of ammo on nothing. Rock smiled. Uncontrolled, hysterical fire. He chucked a softball-size stone about thirty feet to his left. It rustled the leaves of some cottonwoods. Instantly both groups of Reds poured immense firepower onto the offending sapling grove. Little remained of the small stand of foliage when the wall of bullets stopped.

"Fools," screamed the major, who had good cover now behind a dead tree. "Save your ammunition. Fire only when you're fired on." Though the shout was a quick colloquial Russian with a Ukranian inflection, Rockson caught the gist of the order. He had thought this would be easy. Now, with a Red officer in charge, it might be a little harder. The major would have to go.

The Doomsday Warrior took it upon himself to begin crawling down the decline toward the major. With him out of the way there would be no contest. The wet-behind-the-ear soldiers and the drunken insubordinate lieutenant, who had miraculously managed to stay alive behind a solid oak tree's cover, would be easy pickings once the major was taken out.

Rock crawled through the tall grass for a good fifty feet without being detected. Chen had shown him just how to move to appear like the wave of the grain of the fields. When the wind moved the grass, he moved. A wave, undetectable.

He was about to chance attack when he heard the loud concussion of grenades in the approximate position of the Red major. Detroit yelled, "Go for it, man," and jumped up from behind a boulder, throwing another grenade. It sailed over Rockson and impacted just to the left of the major's cover. The Doomsday Warrior ran the fifty feet across the open area and rolled behind a fallen tree. Now he was higher and behind the KGBer. The man knew it and made a run for it. Evidently he was abandoning his half-assed command, heading for the hills. Rock got to his feet and took off after the major. Shots rang out, whizzing by his shoulder, but return fire from his men pinned down the Reds trying to get him. Rock tackled the Blackshirt football style and they fell together in the dust at the top of the hillock.

It was a brief struggle. The man was powerful but

untrained in the martial sciences. Hand-to-hand was not his forte! With a knife to the major's jugular, and the man's arms pinned by Rockson's weight sprawled over him, the major cried, "Surrender! I surrender! Mir!"

Rock knew the Red word for peace. "So it's peace you want. *Mir*, hey?" Rock said, twisting the blade so it made a little red pinprick just to the south of the man's pounding blood vessel. "Well, we'll both get up, then; you tell your men to drop their arms. Okay?"

The major said *"da,"* and they got slowly up. The major was looking for a false move, a way for the tables to be turned, but Rock didn't give him any leeway. With the knife to his throat he walked with Rock back down the hill, shouting, "Surrender. I *order* you to throw down your weapons."

The first group, three men, immediately stood and tossed their rifles and raised their hands. The second group, of three, behind the tree stump, jumped up too, but with their Kalashnikovs blazing as they backed toward the woods. Farrell cut one down with a burst of 9mm slugs.

Archer popped up out of nowhere, his bearlike body moving with grizzly speed. He had threaded a harpoon-size arrow into his steel bow and now let it fly directly at the offending pair of Reds. The arrow, a good four feet of steel with a serrated tip, sliced through the belly of one, and, since his comrade was right behind him, it entered him too—skewering the two of them as they fell face forward, together.

The four surviving Reds—the lieutenant, the major, and two privates—were made to sit with their hands on their heads on the ground. The Free-fighters, who had frisked them quickly for hidden weapons, stood over them.

"How about disposing of this pack of vermin so we can get on with our expedition," said McCaughlin, fingering his Liberator.

"No," Rock replied. "I think we'll let them go on, without weapons or food. These parts are crawling with mountainmen, trappers, all sorts of interesting animals. It's time the KGB learned how to forage, how to hunt, and maybe how to beg the people they come across—people they've been oppressing—for some food, some water."

The major wet his lips with his tongue, and said in broken English, "No! Please. With no weapon, no food, we die."

McCaughlin nudged him with his rifle barrel. "Take your choice, partner. Die now or take your chances. As a matter of fact, Rock, what do you say we take their boots too?"

They all began begging now, and Rock, after a while, said they could keep their boots. They were told to run over the hill, and they did so with just their clothes on their backs.

Farrell put a plastisynth bandage on Rock's nick to prevent infection. In addition to his other skills, the lanky blond man was a pretty fair medic. Somehow that fact hadn't gotten on the file.

As they rode, McCaughlin brought his steed alongside Rockson's and said, "Won't they come back after the little meat we left on the moose? Isn't that giving them too much?"

Rock smiled. "Before we left, I sprinkled it with a

bit of juice from that arovalis plant over at the edge of the field."

McCaughlin laughed. "That will give them a few nightmares." The arovalis, he knew, was a senior cousin of the weed, the stuff that made plains animals as violently mad as rabid dogs if they happened to lunch on it.

Miles beyond the encounter, Rockson called a halt, and they camped, setting up the four survival tents— two men in each. They slept for six hours, except for Archer, who sat watch. The mountainman seemed inexhaustible. But he made up for the sleep he skipped by the huge portions of food he consumed.

They broke camp after McCaughlin had whipped up some moose-a-la moss rations for all of them, with hot coffee. The 'brids, being a much more sturdy species than humans, needed neither rest, nor water, nor warmth. They had been content to chew leaves.

As the first gray light of dawn crept over the frost-covered rolling terrain, Rock saw a high sharp object silhouetted against the sky directly in front of them, about a mile ahead. Rock raised his electron binoculars for a look-see.

"That's the radio antenna," he said. "You men wait here. McCaughlin and I will go ahead on foot to see what's up."

Rock and the big Scotsman walked down the slope of the long hill and, crawling the last hundred yards, stuck their heads over the ridge. They saw the station below, the doors wide open to the morning air, and two lazy men having a siesta, their rifles over their laps as they slept in the warmth emanating from the doorway.

"Tsk, tsk," spat McCaughlin. "So they don't expect visitors. Well, what do you think? Do we slip down right now and take them ourselves, or go back and mount a full-scale attack?"

"Well," Rock said, "we might as well take advantage of the situation. I'd hate to turn down the open-door invitation."

They scurried in a crouch down the slope, and before the guards knew what was up, had them around the necks with knives to their throats. "No noise, pals. Let's go in," said McCaughlin. The frightened Reds savvied the English well enough, and the four of them stepped into the building.

In the large brightly lit room sat six or seven technicians in soiled white smocks. They were unarmed, though rifles were stowed carelessly in a corner.

"Surpriski," McCaughlin said in a loud voice. He and Rockson shoved their hostages face forward onto the floor where they lay motionless, fearful of a fatal bullet in the spine. But none came.

The technicians turned in shock from their tasks monitoring meters and radio equipment around the room. Startled, the men ripped their earphones off and jumped to their feet. Rock swept his Liberator rifle around the room. "Freeze!"

They must have understood, for they did just that. The only breach in the silence came when one dropped his clipboard. He was a tall, lanky young fellow, who evidently knew English.

"Don't shoot. We are unarmed," he pleaded. "We are not soldiers—we are to be evacuated. This place to be shipped out—"

"We just want to use the radio," Rock said softly. "No one will be harmed."

After some coaxing the head tech got the Premier's frequency and handed Rock the mike and headset.

"Rockson calling the Kremlin. Returning Premier Vassily's radio transmission."

The radio crackled out a response, after Rockson repeated the message six times.

"This is the Premier's servant Rahallah," a mellow voice stated.

"Yes, I remember you," Rock said.

"The Premier is napping. I presume you are responding to the message broad-beamed to you in Colorado?"

"Correct, Rahallah. I've got to speak to him," Rock said tersely.

"It will take me a few minutes to wake him and get him to the phone," Rahallah said. "Can you wait?"

Rockson smiled to himself. They were doubtless trying to drag this out so that they could zero in on the location of Century City.

"Save your delaying tactics, Rahallah. I'm at a Red Army radio far away from my home base. Let's be brief. The United States government is pleased that Vassily is going through with his removal of all missiles though we have yet to independently confirm the evacuation is taking place. Assuming that it *is* true, we would like further assistance in tracking Killov and his missiles—using satellite readings or anything else you have to help us."

Vassily's dry, age-cracked voice suddenly came on the line. "Rockson, do you know what time it is in Moscow? Two A.M. But I will speak to you— Rahallah, stay on the extension. We can't give you satellite data on the Killov missiles. You want to know why?" The Premier of all the Soviets laughed bitterly. "Because you destroyed most of our satellites when you blew up the central dome here in Moscow. And even if my jets could locate Killov's white-painted missiles in the snow, Killov would launch them the second he knew he was spotted. But I *can* send you a technician—a Major Scheransky—with a tracking device that can follow Killov's trail on the ground. If you will send a force strong enough to overcome Killov and his estimated one hundred fifty troops, yet sufficiently small to take him by surprise . . ."

Rockson thought for a moment then said, "Have your man para-drop to your radio base—K-23— tomorrow at noon local time. With the missile tracker. But no tricks."

"Somehow, I get the feeling that you don't trust me."

Rockson laughed out loud. "As much as you trust me, Vassily. Once this Killov thing is cleared up, you and I are enemies again. Over and out." He put the mike down. The wide-eyed technicians standing with their hands up along the wall looked awed that Rockson could speak that way to their holy-of-holies.

"He's just a man," said Rock, sensing their mesmerization. "And so am I. And so are you. Put your hands down. Do any of you bastards play poker?

After you all submit to a search, you might want to play a few hundred games with us while we wait together for this Scheransky." The Reds managed to relax a bit. Perhaps they would live, after all.

McCaughlin found that they were eager to learn—and lose at poker. At the end of the first few hours they'd all had ten cups of powerful tea each from a samovar. When they began putting a little vodka in it, the game was forgotten. In Russian and English the conversation began to roam all over the place. It got interesting.

"Freedom, bah," commented one cynical vodka guzzler, the oldest of the techs. "The government—*any* government—is only good for taking your money and sending you or your son to war and for blowing up everybody. The revolutions all start out with good intentions, and then power corrupts. I say, back to nature—Chekhov's ideal of real communal living."

The young one said, "No. In modern times, centralized government is necessary. A dictatorship of the workers—that is what Lenin wanted.

"And," said Rock, "is that what you have?"

"Well, it isn't finalized yet. There are problems."

"You have no checks and balances, kid. The U.S. government always had the Supreme Court, the executive branch, and the legislature—and free press to expose and oppose the power-grabbers. Kept it all aboveboard, whether some politicians wanted it that way or not. All people born equal, but after that . . . they get according to the exertion and ingenuity they put out. From each according to his ability, to each according to his efforts."

"In Communist theory," one of the techs said, "it is: To each according to his needs."

"Sounds like a system for slackers," Rock replied. "Anyway, Communism doesn't even do that. It's all a farce. They use slogans: the workers ruling, freedom of the masses, and all that, and then they do just the opposite."

"True Communism will come—someday," the technician answered. "My government promises me that when the wars are over, socialist man will rise— once and for all."

"Someday, someday," said Rock. "In the meantime everyone is a slave."

Rock had set up the aircraft-detector grid that Schecter's people had supplied. It could even differentiate types of aircraft. It was 11:57 A.M. the next morning when the buzzer went off. One plane. Rockson heaved a sigh of relief and went outside where the rest of the team watched the sky. There—a small Ilyushin N-3A twin-jet—streaking like a knife through the orange clouds and descending slowly to earth.

"Make some more coffee, McCaughlin. And eggs and grits. I'd like to get to know Major Scheransky before we head north with the man."

The parachuter hit the center of a field a hundred yards to the left of the radio station. He was helped out of his harness by Detroit who reached him first, as he seemed to be having a hard time. And no wonder—for the man, a ruddy-faced fellow of about twenty-five, was roly-poly like a big lump of jello. Rock frowned. Is this the man they would take into a frozen hell after a madman like Killov? And where

59

was this goddamn tracking device? Then he heard the plane returning, and he watched as a second chute billowed out.

Scheransky gasped out in near perfect English, "Thanks, comrades! Here comes the antimatter meter." He pointed to the sky.

"I suppose that's the missile tracker?" Rock asked.

"Yes. It's forty kilograms. I didn't want to jump with it. Actually I've never jumped before. It's exhilarating."

"Never jumped before? Are you in the Soviet Army?" Detroit asked. "Aren't you a major?—your insignia says so . . ."

The man flushed. "Well, I work in the lab. I'm a sort of *lab* major. Never had any combat experience. You know—got most of these medals here for inventions of a technical nature."

Rock said, "I see. Well, you'll have to experience a little pain on this trip. I hope you have a strong heart because you'll probably lose a few pounds. Quite a few . . ."

The device floated down and settled perfectly on a thick pile of weeds. "It looks like a tripod-mounted SMG," said McCaughlin.

"But it isn't," said the major. "See? The barrel is solid—uses measuring scopes. I'll have a trace on the radiation of Killov's missiles once you get me to the point they were stolen from—and I can do some initial distance readings."

"Well, man, let's get some breakfast in you and get going," said McCaughlin. "You ever eat wild boar ham and eggs with grits back in Leningrad, pal?"

Over breakfast Rockson introduced the men to the

Red scientist. He addressed the men: "You probably like bringing the major along as little as I do. Russia and the U.S. are enemies and there will be no truce until they are out of America. If this wasn't a necessary joint mission we'd be blasting away at each other. But it *is* a joint mission and I'm sure neither the Premier nor I will go back on our word, at least I won't. And that means *you* won't. Understand—this man is to be protected with your lives!"

"Yes, sir," they answered. But they all eyed Scheransky with suspicion.

Scheransky smiled at them all. "You do as promised—so do I. We find the missiles and deactivate them, send for a team to dismantle them and ship them back to Russia as you rebels agreed. These weapons must be disarmed properly. We can't blow them up; they're antimatter bombs. They explode if strongly impacted. You are familiar, I suppose," he continued, "with the Hiroshima bomb? The one that America dropped on Japan to begin the nuclear terror that still stalks the world?"

"Yeah," Detroit frowned. "We dropped it. It *ended* World War II, buddy. But we didn't *start* World War II. Or World War III." Scheransky's face turned red. He said, "Well, there are many kilograms of antimatter explosive in the missile warhead. Each kilogram of antimatter is ten times more powerful than the Hiroshima bomb. They may well be the most devastating weapons mankind has ever produced. Perhaps this blackie can't understand this, but you can."

Detroit started forward, rage in his eyes. Rockson grabbed the black Freefighter's sleeve and said, "Ease

61

off, man. I want Major Scheransky here to tell us *all* exactly what the destructive potential of these bombs is. You say one kilogram is like ten Hiroshima bombs, Scheransky? So how many kilograms of antimatter are in each warhead that Killov possesses?"

"*That* is a military secret of the Soviet people. I don't have the authority—"

Rockson picked up the Red by the collar and lifted him off the floor. "So you *know*, little scientist. Tell me or I'll let Archer play punching bag with you."

The Soviet scientist looked at Archer, who sat on a nearby desk, bending its legs under his weight.

"One hundred twenty," the lab major shouted out, squirming around.

Rockson dropped the little man. "One hundred twenty kilograms! That means ten times a hundred and twenty."

"My God," shouted Detroit. "That's twelve hundred times the power of the Hiroshima bomb."

The Soviet smiled. "That is correct. Of course, that is per missile—there are five missiles."

Detroit sat down and stared at the table. "How could anyone construct such a deadly thing? Just one of those missiles—could—could—"

Rockson finished his sentence in a soft voice. ". . . Take out a quarter of the state of Colorado!"

In a quiet mood, the men uncrated the antimatter meter. It was about four feet long. "Strange-looking thing," Chen commented.

"And kind of heavy," Rock added, "to drag around

62

with us."

"Yes, heavy," Scheransky said, wiping his sweaty hands on his uniform pants, "but a marvel of Russian technology."

"Damn. We have to lug that thing all the way up into snow country?" said Detroit. "Why, the thing would take a 'brid of its own just to carry it."

"Can't be helped," Rock said. "It's our only way of finding Killov." The Freefighters gingerly set it down alongside the table. The antimatter meter was turned on by the Russian, for demonstration purposes. The long silver cylinder with rows of buttons and meters on it throbbed and pulsed, and then, to their amazement, it started moving. It was turning like a compass needle. It managed this maneuver because it had small ball bearings on its lower side.

"It keeps collecting antimatter traces—meson particles in the air. Normally they don't even exist. If a Meson-5 missile has come by the area within twenty days, the A-M meter should start clicking like a Geiger counter does for any ordinary radiation." The Russian made a proud smile.

"Hey," said Detroit, "look at what was also in the package." He held up a pair of red shiny metal boxes about six inches square and perfectly smooth, one in each hand. "There's more little red boxes out there. Chen's bringing—"

"Be careful," Scheransky shouted in bad English as he stood up, apparently terrified. "Place those down carefully. They are—dangerous."

Detroit placed them gingerly on the floor. They looked harmless enough. "What's in them, Scheransky?"

Scheransky wet his lips and resumed his seat. "They're antimatter drains. They have to be attached to the missiles when we find them, inserted near the warheads. They deplete the antimatter. It's the only way to disarm the warheads. Aside from pulling a few wires in the electrical system, disarming the missiles is child's play. But we have to be very careful placing these 'little red boxes' as you call them next to the warheads. They must be placed in such a way—they are polarized—to reverse the poles . . ."

"But they can't explode by themselves, can they? You said they were 'drains.' How can a drain explode?" Rock asked.

Scheransky smiled. "Antimatter drains have that capability, especially if jarred. Creates the explosive force of a hand grenade. The technical explanation is quite—"

"We'll handle them gently from now on. Detroit, why don't you go tell Chen before he starts juggling the last red boxes."

"Will do." Detroit exited with all due haste.

"Now," Scheransky said, putting his pale hands back flat on the table, "I volunteered for this mission. I hope you understand there will be—there *must* be no failure on your part, Rockson, to help me deactivate the missiles. They are not to be merely captured. The agreement is that the missiles will be returned to their owner—the Soviet Empire."

"We don't need or want your fucking missiles. We're winning without nuclear weapons, or anti-matter weapons. Because we have freedom on our side. Vassily knows that we'll never use weapons of mass destruction. History has taught us that's a shortcut to hell. *We* want this planet to survive. *My* side will go through with the agreement."

Scheransky eyed this strange bronze-skinned mutant American. He stared into the mismatched violet-aqua eyes. He had been told Rockson was exceptional—and he was.

"I will tell you what you need to know to help disarm the missiles, Rockson, just in case something happens to me. We must make haste. If we lose Killov, we might not be able to pick up his trail. We must never be more than ten days behind him. Nine to be safe."

"Doesn't this meson radiation the missiles give out hurt people?" Rock asked. "That might be good to know."

"No. It passes right through the body. And it's likely to imbed itself into the ground or ice below the trucks as they pass. The A-M meter *works*. I've tried it in Siberia, when we lost one of the missiles being transported by air. Led us right to the crash spot." He bit his lips.

"So," said Rockson, "you have more of these babies. Vassily said there were only these five."

"No. There was one other, also being transported to Idaho—the Premier was afraid they would explode by themselves, which is theoretically conceivable, though unlikely. He didn't want them on Soviet soil if . . ." Scheransky trailed off and looked at the floor. "Anyway," he mumbled, "the sixth missile was damaged beyond repair and deactivated by one of those red boxes over there on the floor." He looked up again. "I am telling the truth."

Now it was the Doomsday Warrior's turn to assess

the man before him. He decided to trust Scheransky—for now. He had a hunch this wasn't the worst Red he'd ever run into. He was a scientist; his eyes bespoke real intelligence and thought. He lacked the hard eyes Rock had seen so often in Russian officers. But he'd keep an eye on him anyway. Rockson knew that Vassily was likely to double-cross them, if he could.

Chapter 6

It had been a routine flight from Moscow for the returning Russian President of the United States. With the traces of his last meal having just been cleared away, Zhabnov absentmindedly took a sip of bourbon. The three ice cubes tinkled reassuringly in his glass. His escape flight to Moscow a month earlier hadn't been so pleasant. He'd *warned* Vassily repeatedly that Killov was getting too powerful, but Vassily had been preoccupied with his damned books. When the inevitable happened, and Killov's KGB Blackshirts stormed Washington, Zhabnov had the cunning and foresight to have a chopper pilot on twenty-four-hour alert on the back lawn of the White House ready to carry him to a Mach 5 jet waiting on a hidden runway.

Even then, he'd barely escaped the jaws of Killov, the Skull.

A single tear came into each eye as he thought of his loyal palace guards who'd bravely fought the KGB Commandos. He really must raise a monument

67

to them. They'd laid their lives on the line and had been sacrificed so that he might be saved. Oh, how he had wanted to stay in Washington and fight, but it was of paramount importance that he, the logical successor to the pinnacle of Red Power, survive. The twelve men of his field staff that he'd magnanimously allowed aboard his escape jet understood his importance. The long flight back to Moscow had been filled with toasts of his heroism and brilliance in preparing the daring escape.

But he had been amazed, when he arrived in Moscow, that he didn't get a hero's welcome—a red carpet, an award ceremony. *No.* He'd been met with jeers, been called a yellow coward by Vassily himself. His reward had been pushing papers in the Kremlin under the watchful eye of Vassily's black servant, Rahallah, whom he loathed even more than the paperwork. For four weeks that voodoo priest had made him feel like a slave, a lackey. Imagine he, Zhabnov, President of the U.S.S.A., doing mere clerical work under a blackie; his mind was meant for greater things. Leadership. Management of the Red forces of the entire U.S.S.A. And with his uncle Vassily lingering on his deathbed, it was only a matter of time before he would run the world. When news reached Moscow that the KGB troops occupying Washington had been defeated by the combined attacks of Red and American troops, Vassily had finally relented and given Zhabnov permission to return.

He looked out the jet's window and watched the sun streaming through the clouds, forming canyons as great as those of the Grand Canyon. He marveled that up here he was privy to the sun's first rays while the earth below was still enveloped in darkness. He loved heights. The ascent after takeoff had been glorious. He'd felt as if he were a bird able to fly with his own wings. . . . His wings may have been clipped in Moscow, but now once again he was a soaring eagle. He, Supreme President of the U.S.S.A., was flying to reclaim his birthright, his destiny.

His reverie was suddenly interrupted by a flashing light above his seat and the sound of the pilot's voice intoning, "Fasten your seat belt, sir. We're approaching Washington." This was the part he hated. Zhabnov squirmed deeper into his specially designed seat, wide enough for two ordinary men, and struggled to fasten the seat belt over his protruding belly. He hated descents. He was always afraid the jet would crash. Over and over he'd been given flying statistics which indicated that fewer accidents happened in the air than on the ground. But although he loved statistics, he knew only too well how easily they could be manipulated. He hadn't been above such things himself.

The two glasses of bourbon were provided for him, as he had ordered. One for each fist. He gulped them both down and his knuckles grew white as he gripped the armrests in his hands. He clenched his teeth and closed his eyes tight like steel doors—so if death came, he wouldn't have to see it.

The sun was just coming over the horizon as the Soyuz Stratocruiser landed at Lenin International Airport. The sleek supermodern eight-engine jet, equipped with the most advanced Russian computerized technology, landed like a living thing. Its wheels seemed to reach for the ground like claws. The pilot lowered the wing flaps and the engines reversed. Zhabnov opened his eyes in time to see the blur outside his window turn into hangars and ramps as the jet slowed to a taxiing speed down the runway. Zhabnov was back in Washington.

He unbuckled his seat belt. At last he could get its annoying pressure off his stomach. Not only did it bother his belly, but it crushed the jacket of his bright olive uniform. He detested frumpiness. He was a spit-and-polish man. He wiped the nervous sweat off his oily countenance with a handkerchief and smoothed the few wisps of blond hair across his scalp in the reflection of his pocket mirror. He'd have to look his best for the brass-band reception that was surely waiting for him now that Killov had been routed out of Washington; out of the U.S.S.A. for that matter. The thought of Killov being on the run like a hunted animal caused Zhabnov to lick his lips with great satisfaction.

The plane came to a halt. Zhabnov peered anxiously through his window for the crowd. They must be on the other side of the plane, he thought. He stood up and threw his shoulders back and sucked in his gut. Sticking his cap under his arm he strode purposefully to the exit. It came as a shock when he descended the staircase with four guards that no one was there to greet him. Not a soul.

Zhabnov put his hand to his eyes to block out the morning sun's rays and stared off into the distance. Maybe he was early? He dimly perceived a moving object coming down the runway to meet him. It was one long, low black vehicle—the White House Zil

70

limo, with his presidential colors flying. His disappointment was pushed aside by the thought that it must be for his security, national security, that the runway had been cleared, that the crowds had been forced to disperse. Yes, that was it. It's better that way. Safer.

No sooner was Zhabnov seated than the door was slammed shut and the driver floored the pedal. The Zil limo with its presidential colors waving madly was off like a shot from a cannon and Zhabnov was thrown back against the seat.

They raced over the mighty Potomac on the Arlington Memorial Bridge and drove past the Lincoln Memorial. It was still there—unscathed. But that was more than Zhabnov could say about the rest of the mall. It looked as if a titanic tornado had passed through. Zhabnov gasped. Instead of the fall foliage he had expected to see, the cherry trees were almost bare. Some were twisted as if by a giant hand, uprooted and then tossed on the mall. Other trees were leaning precariously over the gray choppy Tidal Basin. The remaining ones were split open showing their open wounds—broken, dead limbs were everywhere. The Washington Monument appeared cracked and crooked, as if it were about to topple. There was only twisted rubble where the Octagon prison had stood.

They raced past the ellipse, where Zhabnov got his first good look at the White House. Even from the car, Zhabnov could see that his weatherproof plastic dome above the Capitol and grounds had been shattered. His foot-thick, transparent, three-hundred-foot high, impenetrable, plastisynth weather

71

dome that he had built for security around the Presidential mansion had been smashed into shards. The entire East Wing was a shambles; and the West Wing had been utterly destroyed. KGB choppers had ground his roses to a pulpy red paste as they'd landed by the South Portico. His children. His creations. His precious genetically spliced hybrid stock of roses had been wiped out. He might never be able to recreate them. He, who had won top prize every year in the Taskent Rose Competition for his *Rosa familiaris cruxae* and American Beauty Roses among others, wouldn't even be able to enter this year. Might never be able to show his face at the Taskent Horticultural Show again.

The Zil limo sped down the driveway from Pennsylvania Avenue through the White House gate which hung open askew on one hinge. The White House lawn was nothing but torn-up earth, as if an earthquake had hit. The Zil limo screeched to a halt outside the White House steps. Zhabnov got out of the limo in a daze. No one was on the sidewalk to greet him. He walked up to the rubble-strewn steps. The blackened wood door to the entrance was locked. He rang the bell but there was no response. How humiliating that the President of the U.S.S.A. was actually banging on his own door to be let in, he thought, enraged. Heads would roll.

Finally, after what seemed like an eternity, the door was opened by a frail woman carrying a bucket of sudsy water and a mop. "Who are you?" she asked in a weak voice.

"I'm me, the President of the U.S.S.A.," Zhabnov responded.

"President Zhabnov isn't here. He's in Russia."

"I'm not *asking* for him, I *am* him," Zhabnov screamed.

"Him who?"

"Him! I am President Zhabnov."

"I told you already, he isn't here."

"I'm President Zhabnov," he shouted, growing red from neck to forehead.

Suddenly a pale, bespeckled face appeared wearing a perplexed blank expression, which widened into a look of astonishment. "President Zhabnov!" the pale man exclaimed in the thin shrill voice that usually set Zhabnov's teeth on edge.

Zhabnov shouted, "Gudonov!" and greeted his male secretary with a bear hug. Never had he dreamed he would be so thankful to see a familiar and hated face.

Gudonov didn't know what to make of this hearty, emotional bearhug. He felt as if his bones were being crushed, and Zhabnov's breath was steaming up his glasses.

Zhabnov recovered his poise. He abruptly stepped away from Gudonov, his shoulders back, and raising himself to his full height, he bellowed, "What is the meaning of all this? Where is everyone?"

"You weren't expected until tomorrow morning," Gudonov gasped, trying to get back his wind. "Things are damaged. I hoped—"

Zhabnov gazed about him. Paint hung from the ceiling in strips. Plaster had fallen from the walls and ceiling. The burned ragged curtains hung in frayed tatters. Buckets had been placed everywhere. He raised his eyebrows.

"The roof has been badly damaged by the KGB attack and the buckets are there to catch the leaks," Gudonov explained to the unasked question. "As you can see, there is only a skeleton crew on duty since so much of the White House has been destroyed . . ."

"Show me, Gudonov," the fat, jowly man ordered.

Gudonov took Zhabnov on a quick tour of his "palace." The presidential office was a mess. Its shiny white paint was water-spotted, and the charcoal gray smudges gave evidence of a fire. Zhabnov's floor-to-ceiling purple velvet drapes had been torn and they sagged to the floor. The veneer of his immense cherry-topped desk inlaid with the presidential seal was charred. The figure of a skull and the initial *K* was carved into its surface. Killov! The vandal! His suite of Empire salon furniture, recently upholstered in an eagle design of blue and gold, was faded, threadbare, and frazzled. The balcony hung precariously, as if by a prayer. The ten-foot-high mirror that hung between the portraits of Washington and Lincoln had been smashed.

"Where are the portraits?" Zhabnov asked, staring at the dark squares along the wall where the pictures should have been.

"In the basement," replied Gudonov. "The portraits were removed during the KGB occupation for safekeeping."

As they went on their way to the basement, a thin wisp of hope rose in Zhabnov's mind. Maybe the Stuart portrait of Washington had been destroyed? He certainly hoped so. Vassily would never let him dispose of the damned thing! The basement smelled

74

musty, dusty, and stale. They toured the basement and found that the presidential pictures were in good order. Stuart's painting had survived, intact. Zhabnov was let down. He hated that portrait. It reminded him of a cadaver come back from the grave, and its eyes always seemed accusing or at least disapproving. He was worried about the priceless paintings—his own collection of twentieth-century masterpieces. They came at last to his precious Keane painting, "Big Eyed Tears." It had been gored through. Slashed. It was as if someone had tried to kill the portrait of the young girl-child with immense eyes and innocent mouth, holding a single rose. The tear that hung from her right eye seemed to express her agony. This was too much. Zhabnov broke down into tears.

Zhabnov sobbed as he blew his nose. An anger arose in his breast unlike any he'd known before. Those who had defiled his Keane painting, crushed his precious roses into red paste, would be made to pay. They would be made to feel the thorn of the rose.

Yes, what a good idea. He would find them and have them wrapped in thorn bushes—their entire bodies punctured ten thousand times by the inch-long spikes. It would take them so very long to die.

Chapter 7

The next five days of the Freefighters' expedition were uneventful. Rockson, fearing a trap, had the team ride to a spot fifty miles north of the Idaho-5 base, to intersect the only road north, old Interstate 15, outside Pocatello, Idaho. They'd try to pick up Killov's trail there.

Scheransky and Rock already had one argument—Scheransky saying the whole party could be helped along by Sov regular troops, and Rock saying no dice, they were going on their own.

Then, at the crossing of the Snake River—it was fordable just outside of Blackfoot—Scheransky put up a fuss about the necessity of keeping Vassily informed by radio of their progress.

"Forget it," Rock said. The team had a shortwave radio that they could reach Century City with in case of emergency—in case the missiles were found—but he sure as hell didn't want to use it. "We'll contact Vassily *after* we achieve our objective. He'll get no goddamned progress reports."

At last they reached the grass and cracks of Route I-15, just fifty miles from the base from which the missiles had been stolen.

Scheransky, grumbling, set up the tracking device and in a matter of minutes it began beeping. "If we just follow the road . . . he's probably taken it straight into Canada," Scheransky said. "See? The tracker turned once, then points down the road."

"How old is the trace?" Rock asked. "Can you tell?"

"Sure—he was here, oh, a week ago—seven or eight days . . ."

They found deep tracks in the mud-splattered highway—huge convoy trucks with twenty-four-inch tires carrying their loads of death north. "No need for further readings for a while, Major.

"Let's follow the footprints," Rock said, staying his 'brid. "They always lead to the beast that made them."

The moon swept up into the deep purple sky after sundown. Its gibbous elegance lit the rolling road before them with waves of white. On this night it looked so cold, so untouchable against the radioactive glowing atmosphere of the earth, striated with endlessly orbiting webs of pink and green strontium clouds.

High atop his 'brid, Ted Rockson surveyed the scene with his piercing mismatched eyes. Behind, the rest of the expeditionary attack force rode in silence. Magnificent, Rock thought to himself, gazing up at the perfect symmetry of the moon and stars, the violet clouds that floated over it all. For a moment it created a vision of ultimate beauty, a Japanese print spread out across the cold heavens. Beautiful, *but* . . . Those heavens, those clouds, were filled with radioactive elements, atoms whose superhot nuclei would produce death rays for thousands of years.

As he shifted in his saddle, Rockson patted his big mutant horse on the neck. It seemed a little skittish tonight. It knew—all the 'brids sensed when they were going out on a mission. Sometimes when his faint ESP powers were particularly keen, Rockson could read the thoughts of the big steeds—their strength, their simple needs, their devotion to man.

The faces of Kim and Rona kept interfering with the stars above him. Their faces covered with blood, their shrieking as the Red missiles dug deep into Century City's tunnels and exploded, melting flesh, memory, flashed in his mind. The fearsome image kept burning in his head. He gritted his teeth together, gazed past the strontium clouds, beyond the bands of pink and green, writhing like luminescent gargoyles far above, gazed on past the moon, beyond the stars. He searched and probed with all his heart for a God that he wasn't even sure existed, and pleaded with him to spare Century City.

Keeping a slow, even gait, they rode on through the cool night, letting the 'brids set the pace. They'd have to go slowly—the road was now bumpy, pitted, but Rock didn't want to be behind schedule when the sun came up.

In the morning, the tired riders saw the big wheel-tracks veer off the road and continue overland. Heading straight north.

At last they hit the Great North Prairie, and the 'brids were able to pick up speed through the frost-tinged fields of sunflowers, dandelions, and clover. Edging his smaller 'brid near Rock, Detroit came up to the lead. He smiled, as if to say, It's great to be on a mission with you. The bull-necked man had accompanied Rockson on many missions—each more dangerous than the one before. But they had always made it through, usually against the kind of odds a local high-school team would have had against the Chicago Bears.

Detroit was the finest example of an intelligent, skilled soldier of freedom, and was a real gentleman, as well as the most loyal of friends. The mangling of his arm a few months earlier had made Detroit even more ready to fight America's enemies.

"Maybe we're starting to get a bit too old for this sort of thing," the black Freefighter said with a laugh as he looked over at Rockson, seeking a rise. He didn't mean it.

"C'mon dude. We're never too old for a battle. May as well die with our boots on," Rock replied, winking.

"I like my battles in *warm* weather." Detroit laughed.

"Say, how's the arm?" Rock asked. "I know the docs said it would take some months to come into full use, but I was hoping . . ." Detroit's arm had been operated on in Century City's hospital, replaced with a bionic counterpart.

"Better than ever," Detroit said, raising it and twisting it around. "I was having some difficulty with the elbow for a while. Needed oil! Feels great now. I've been working on my grenade chucking and I'm already past my old status. Fastballs at 135 mph. Grenades heaved over five hundred feet."

Detroit, besides being armed with the Liberator automatic rifle that Century City manufactured and shipped out to other free cities, always carried fifteen to twenty grenades in bandoliers strapped across his massive chest. Grenades armed to explode, to send out waves of burning phosphorus or stun gas. The ebony Freefighter was a one-man army toting his own portable arsenal.

The two compatriots rode on quietly for a while, enjoying the early-morning breezes and arias of winter birds singing their happy greetings. The world could be beautiful at times. The tall ice-coated prairie-grass stalks glowed silver in the slanting sun. The manes of their steady steeds caught the same light and reflected it gold or tan.

But Detroit was uneasy. "Will we get Killov, finally?" he asked.

Rock was thoughtful for a moment, then answered, "He's human. We'll get him. Never think otherwise, Detroit."

The easily visible tire tracks through the prairie took them to the 49th parallel—the old dividing line between the U.S. and Canada. The temperature fell, the sun was blotted by clouds of snow swirling in the bitter winds. The Geiger counter was clicking a bit—residue radioactivity from the silos in north Idaho that were hit a hundred years earlier by incoming Red missiles. Rock knew that was why nothing grew here except crabgrass—spiky sharp spines jutting from the thickening snow.

Upon Rockson's command, the tracker was set up again and it beeped and spun. Scheransky said excitedly, "Killov has come through here five days ago. The reading is quite definite!"

"We're gaining on the bastard," McCaughlin said, with some joy. "And just look at the hills ahead—great for animals but hell for a convoy of heavy trucks." Though the trucks' thick ruts were now obscured by the deepening snow, the A-M tracker showed the way. A marker sign dangled to the side, barely legible: WELCOME TO CANADA, it offered. Rockson set his face against the wind. His 'brid stepped over a rusty line on some concrete pavement. Rock saw a collapsed booth. A checkpoint—with nothing to check anymore.

The team headed into Canada. The way was more gullied now. Occasionally they could see the snow-muted tracks of the big wheels of Killov's trucks, like the preserved tracks of some creature from the Pleistocene Era.

Rockson had that old feeling again: the mutant's sixth sense. It told him that they were being *watched*.

Chapter 8

That same afternoon, exhausted from his rounds, Zhabnov was propped up on his featherbed in the master bedroom of the White House. "Take this down," Zhabnov ordered. Gudonov, who was standing by, reached for the gold pen, dangling by a thin chain from his lapel so that he wouldn't lose it. He grabbed his pad, similarly attached, ready to add to the already lengthy list of repairs Zhabnov had ordered. "I want you to round up a team of art experts to scour the land, search every museum and art collection for undiscovered Keane paintings. Notify me as soon as they're assembled," Zhabnov added as he dismissed Gudonov with a wave of his hand.

As soon as Gudonov had left the room and closed the door behind him, Zhabnov's stomach sagged. The effort of holding himself in was always a strain. The Red President gazed about the room after he changed into his pajamas. Even here in his room, Zhabnov couldn't escape the ravages of the White House. Buckets were placed strategically on his nightstand, bureau, and floor to catch the constant leaks. His carpet was water stained and his purple velvet curtains drooped. It was not a fit room for a leader such as he.

He stared at the emptiness of his king-size bed. He was alone. No nubile young maiden awaited him to ease the cares and woes of the past horrid hours. He slid between the cold damp sheets and stared vacantly at the darkened square that should have held his greatest portrait. He thought again of Keane's masterpiece, "Big Eyed Tears," and began to sob. He reached for his covers.

He clutched the pillow tightly to his chest as if for protection and drifted to sleep. . . . Vague thoughts of flying bats filled his mind. He fell into dreams. He was being caressed by a beautiful young girl—naked. He fondled his pillow as he dreamed that she handed him a single perfect rose. He reached to take it, but it turned to red paste that dripped down her body. A big tear appeared in her eye and was followed by another and another. The tears turned to blood and soaked the bed, seeping through to the floor.

The bed groaned and creaked as Zhabnov tossed and turned. Deeper and deeper in dream . . . The bed fell through the floor down to the basement. He got out of bed and winced as his bare feet hit the clammy basement floor and shuddered as a damp icy chill spread through his body. A chill he could feel to his bones. An army of skeletons assembled to mop up the blood that oozed through the ceiling, wringing their mops out in pails. He walked over to the nearest skeleton and demanded to know what was happening.

"Who are you?" asked the skeleton, its fleshless jaws hanging agape.

"I am President of the U.S.S.A.," Zhabnov croaked in fear and anger.

"You're not the President," said another, its jawbone dropping until it dangled, held only by a gold chain.

Zhabnov stepped back aghast and watched in horror as the skeleton retrieved its jaw and set it back in its place.

"*He* is President," the skull said, pointing to the left. Zhabnov followed the long bony finger to where it was pointing until his eyes came to rest on Stuart's portrait of Washington.

"But he's dead!" Zhabnov protested.

"Not in spirit," said a ghostly voice that echoed through the basement.

"Who said that?" Zhabnov shuddered nervously.

"I did," the voice replied with an icy tone. Zhabnov noticed the painting's eyes move.

"I think that Stuart managed to grasp the essence of my spirit, don't you?" asked the painting. Now Zhabnov saw Washington's lips move.

"This can't be," Zhabnov stammered. "You're only a portrait. I must be losing my mind to be talking to a painting."

"Actually, we've been expecting you," said Washington, parting his lips in a hideous, toothless grin of bloody gums.

Zhabnov gasped, as a misty face was beginning to emerge from the picture. He nearly screamed when the pulsing phantom of Washington stepped slowly out of the portrait and onto the cold floor beside him.

He put his hands over his face.

"I've done nothing to you. I even kept your painting," he protested.

"Look at me," the phantom commanded. In spite of himself, Zhabnov peered through his fingers. The now-solid-appearing apparition had a ghastly pallor tinged with a faint flush of fever. The accusing eyes were of an unearthly luminosity. His clothing was faded and decayed as if eaten by worms, and hung around the thing in tatters.

"My spirit has been troubled by your presence in my nation's hallowed halls. It is your disturbance of this place that has summoned me from my grave," he accused, pointing a trembling finger in Zhabnov's face.

"I didn't do anything," Zhabnov whimpered.

"Oh but you did," the hideous spirit of Washington intoned. "You've come and taken over my country, my people. You may think that the power is on your side because of your weapons and troops—but we, the dead, have our eyes on you, Zhabnov. We're reaching for you to bring you down into our world."

Everywhere around the room, the walls began to glow. Spirits of other Presidents came through the walls and began flying around Zhabnov like a tornado—the eyes glowing, the black holes of mouths, chanting like the dismal choruses of hell.

"Zhabnov—we've come for you. Zhabnov, Zhabnov, we want you, we want you." They jabbed at Zhabnov with skeletal hands from the grave.

"No, no, no!" Zhabnov pleaded, shaking his head.

He awoke in a sweat, wrapped like a mummy in

86

the sheets, his face under the pillow. He gasped for air.

"President Zhabnov, President Zhabnov," said Gudonov in his shrill, piercing voice, tapping him vigorously.

Throwing the pillow off, Zhabnov groaned.

"Wake up! You have an important telephone call."

It was from Denkov, the general in charge of the attack on the Denver Monolith—the KGB's last known toehold in the country. Denkov's raspy Ukrainian-peasant voice reported, "Sir, the siege is going well."

"When will you wipe out the enemy?" Zhabnov asked. "I could use you back here."

Denkov, never a rash man, paused. The siege had actually bogged down. The KGB troops, even without Killov's leadership, were fighting tooth and nail.

"Well?" Zhabnov shouted. "When?"

"A few days, a week."

"Do it faster."

Chapter 9

It was a gray day, the kind of day on which a man thinks of dying. White broiling clouds overhead discharged a steady heavy snow that blanketed their way and made visibility nil. Rockson kept the men moving through the deeper and deeper drifts. They leaned low on their thick-maned 'brids, using the pungent mops of dark golden mane as blankets, and zipped up their nylon super-insulated parkas. The Doomsday Warrior noticed that the treetops of the occasional evergreens they passed were starting to wave back and forth. That was bad. A blow was coming, maybe a big one—the first signs of an Arctic blizzard, with untold feet of snow waiting to drop on the team.

As the 'brids stumbled on and the temperature dropped, the skies above grew dimmer and dimmer, as if it were night though it was only one in the afternoon. "Men," he turned and shouted, "we'll have to make camp soon. Keep your eyes peeled for any kind of shelter and—"

He paused in midsentence as he suddenly saw faint shapes at the limits of his vision through the falling snow. "Halt," Rock said in a lower voice to his men. The men stopped their 'brids in their tracks. For a moment, but for the snorting of their steeds all was silent, and then—yells and dog barks. Rockson located the direction of the dim noises off to his left and lifted Schecter's haze-cutting electron binoculars out of the case putting them to his eyes. The binoculars, as he scanned the horizon, automatically adjusted their forty-power focus, and within seconds he saw the source of the disturbance. Dog sleds and drivers—and they were heading this way.

"Defensive positions, men," Rock shouted. "Take advantage of the terrain. Get over behind those frost buckles to the side of the road."

Rock could hear the shouts of the strangers now, as he left his 'brid and dove belly down behind a slight protuberance in the drifting snow. He could hear the cracks of whips as the drivers pushed their teams to maximum speed. They were coming in fast.

There were a dozen sleds approaching with five or six men trailing each on skis, pulled along by ropes attached to the laden sleds—rifles slung over their shoulders or cradled in their arms. Through the electron binoculars' crisp laser-enhanced images he could see the expressions on the Mongol-stock faces—and they didn't look friendly. The Freefighters waited, motionless in the snow, Liberator rifles steady in their hands, waiting. They were upon them. A lead sled skidded to a halt and the first five men approached, the others staying a bit back.

Rock stepped forward, indicating he was the

leader. Rifles trained on rifles, but at least they hadn't come in shooting.

The leader pulled down his parka top of fur and sealskin and raised his empty hand. Rock raised his hand in the same universal gesture.

The man stepped five paces forward as Rock waited, his hand ready to go for his quick-draw holster and the .12-gauge pistol that lay inside.

"Hello," the leather-faced man said, "why do you come this way? Are you Canadians? Do you speak English?"

"We're Americans," Rock said, "Freedom fighters." He did not attempt to be evasive. Most people he had come across in nuke-devastated North America had a universal and deep hatred of the Russians. He had yet to run across a group who hadn't heard of the American Freefighters and who weren't at least neutral to their cause.

The man's shoulders seemed to relax. He said, "That is good, if you are who you say you are." The man did not come forward to shake hands, though. He cradled a long-range .50-caliber World War III rifle that looked like it could take out a whale with a single shot. "And who are you?"

"Name's Ted Rockson, but you may know me as—"

"The Doomsday Warrior?" the man laughed bitterly and spat in the snow. "That's impossible. The Doomsday Warrior is seven feet tall, at least. He is much more muscular than you are, and has a voice like thunder. But you are the leader of this group that trespasses on the North Range—our land— Why do you trespass?"

"We are in pursuit of Russians who have stolen equipment that we want back—dangerous equipment that could destroy all your people in a flash. Have you seen these Russians? They might not have worn regular Soviet uniforms."

"Yes—yes, we have," the man said slowly and deliberately. "They came through five days ago—we tried to be friendly to them. In return, they killed five of my people. They stole much food and supplies. How do we know you are Americans and not Russians also?"

"And who am *I* addressing?" Rock asked with a sigh, somehow not in the mood to prove his trustworthiness.

"Tinglim, Chief of the Nara-Eskimos. King of the Aurora. Lord of the tundra south of the Sasquatch River.

"Well, Mr. Tinglim," Rock said, "can your men put down their rifles, and mine will do the same? Find it hard to carry on a conversation with guns poking out of everywhere."

Tinglim said something in a language Rockson didn't know, and the Eskimos lowered their rifles. Rock ordered his team to follow suit.

"Again, I ask you—What is your real name, mister?" Tinglim demanded. Rockson repeated his claim. Some of the Eskimos laughed. But Rock pulled down his hood and they stopped.

Tinglim stepped forward. "Hummmm. You have the multicolored eyes and the streak of white hair the legend speaks of, but you are not seven feet tall, maybe just six feet. No, you can't be him." He turned and animatedly repeated his remarks in Nara lingo.

The dark-faced men laughed coarsely. Then he shouted something. From the most distant sled a figure stepped forward—a figure of enormous girth swaddled in furs. A man-monster, seven feet tall at least, his hands were chained together—and he strode like he owned the world. The Eskimos made a wide path for him. He came up alongside Tinglim and dwarfed the big man.

"This is Olmo, our slave. We captured this wild man last year. Sometimes we pit him against the fighters of other tribes. We win much food, much ammunition," he laughed.

"Pleased to meet you," Rockson said.

The man snorted, like a bull, and glared down with nothing but hate in the almond-shaped eyes.

"I don't believe you are who you say you are," the Eskimo chief said. "And that means you are probably lying about everything. If you were the Doomsday Warrior you could defeat Olmo in hand-to-hand battle . . ."

"Well, sorry to disappoint you," Rock said, "but I'm not in the mood to fight anyone today. Nevertheless, I *am* the Doomsday Warrior. And we are Freefighters."

"You are *not* Freefighters!" Tinglim snapped. "Olmo will battle you, and if you are the Doomsday Warrior you will defeat him."

The Nara chief shouted orders and rifles swung up. So did the Freefighters' weapons.

"You will all die," Tinglim sneered. "We are many. You are few. If you do not wish to die, you must fight Olmo. Truth will win."

It was fight-or-die time again. Rockson had been

in this situation too much lately. It didn't pay to have a reputation, he mused as the Eskimos unchained the oversized champion.

"Any rules?" Rock asked, taking off his jacket.

The Nara were turning their sleds sideways, commanding their huskies to lie down as they settled back for a good show.

"What are the rules?" Rock asked again.

"No guns," Olmo snarled, shucking his sealskin jacket, stripping down to his hulking bare chest. The man was like a sumo wrestler, but more muscled—and covered with thick brown hair. He hardly looked human. And with his face twisted up in a snarl, lips curled back over jagged teeth . . . Rock felt as if he were facing something from a prehistoric age.

Olmo took off his boots and threw them over his shoulder. Rock kept his combat snow-cleats on, and his clothes—the air was frigid. They started circling each other; cries of support and suggestions began coming from both sides. Olmo shot in close and suddenly came forward, feet first, attempting to snare Rock's legs, twisting him down into the snow. Now he had the advantage of his enormous girth, muscles, and weight, and gripped the Doomsday Warrior around the neck in a hammerlock of death—but Rockson somehow twisted and slipped free. He pulled out his long hunting blade and held it forward. Rock wasn't about to duke it out with something this powerful and fast. The half-animal murder machine was thrown a harpoon by a Nara man. He caught it and smiled a jagged smile of menace.

As quick as a cat he leapt forward, thrusting the

harpoon at Rockson's stomach. Rock saw the flicker of the killer's eyes and knew the weapon was coming. The Doomsday Warrior jumped to the side and swung the sharp edge of his hunting knife at Olmo's abdomen. The blade barely made contact as the man was able to stop his great bulk in mid-stride. Still, Rock's blade drew a thin line of blood along the giant's stomach. The man-thing pulled back a few feet and looked at the American with surprise. No man had ever cut him in his thirty years of life. And they had fought the most famous fighters of many tribes!

The maddened fighter opened his jaws, showing his bent rows of broken teeth. He made what Rock could only interpret as a smile, though hardly a friendly one.

"Good fight," Olmo snarled. "Now me kill."

Rock and Olmo, now having tested one another, squared off circling each other slowly. The Eskimo's slave-fighter was more wary now. He knew this was not an ordinary man, not an ordinary fighter. He felt no fear—just caution. He would win, of that there was no doubt. For he had many tricks.

Rock hefted his knife at chest level, moving it from side to side ready for whatever attack Olmo chose. He had decided to let the Arctic monster do the attacking—he would counterattack. The man was too big for Rock to go in—let him make the first move.

Olmo feinted to the right. As Rockson responded he twisted and came at the American's side with the harpoon. The razor-sharp tip grazed Rock's ribs, gouging out half an inch of flesh, but not penetrating the rib cage. As the weapon slid past his body, Rockson lashed out with a spinning sidekick to the thing's groin. It caught Olmo squarely in the groin and nearly lifted the howling monster off the snow.

The kick took the wind from the thing, and he landed sitting, his weapon falling to the side. Rockson moved in slashing with his knife, but Olmo leaped up and out of the way, circling to the left now, retrieving the harpoon. The big man-thing opened his immense hands and closed them slowly, like he had Rockson's head in each baseball-mitt-sized appendage. The crushing power the hands had could flatten a man's skull! Rock sensed that the move was to distract him and detected a slight repositioning of Olmo's feet.

The giant broad-jumped through the air at the Doomsday Warrior, who leapt to the side. As the Doomsday Warrior moved, the Eskimo champion heaved the harpoon at an amazing speed. Rockson twisted desperately and the harpoon just missed. It flew by, landing twenty yards away where it stuck a foot deep in the snow. The giant came at him with a mad look on his distorted hairy face. He would crush the frail man with his huge arms. Rockson mightily threw his knife dead-center, not into the body, but into the forehead of his murderous adversary. He rolled to the side as the man-thing plunged on to where he had just been. Olmo, the razor-sharp knife imbedded in his thick skull, fell forward, splashing red on the white snow, his hands jerking spasmodically. Rockson had thrown with all his might, so that the tip of the hunting blade stuck out of the shattered rear of the head—matted hair dripping brown brain fluid and red blood onto the whiteness of the northern plains. That was that.

Rockson turned toward his men, but he saw something wrong. The men's expressions were those of horror. Rockson spun and found Olmo was standing again, his eyes half bulging out, blood pouring from his mouth. He staggered forward spitting red. Immense arms again sought for Rockson. With a knife right through his head, still he stumbled on. Maybe the damned thing didn't even need a brain.

"Here, Rock," said Detroit, tossing him one of the harpoons they'd brought from Century City. Rock caught it.

Rockson circled the dying monstrosity for a few seconds and then suddenly jammed the harpoon straight into the monster's gut. He twisted its jagged serrated edge back out, trailing guts with it. Olmo staggered backward looking at the Freefighter in bewilderment. His legs trembled violently as they tried to hold up the quarter ton of weight. Rockson stared at the half-human mutant and wished it had all been different. The man was cruel. But he was brave as well. If he had been with the Freefighters he would have made a hell of a warrior. But such was not to be his fate.

The Doomsday Warrior jabbed the harpoon forward again with a sudden and powerful motion. It went into Olmo's hairy throat clear through his neck. Olmo's eyes rolled up. The giant tottered and then, face forward, Olmo slammed into the red-caked snow. The most feared of the fighters of the North had met his match—Ted Rockson, the Doomsday Warrior.

"You *are* the Doomsday Warrior!" Tinglim said, falling to his knees and touching his hands together in front of him as if in prayer. "Excuse me for doubting you, God Rockson."

"I'm no damn god—stand up, man! I've had to kill Olmo because you think Rockson is a god, not a man. Now you must help me—help *us* defeat Killov and his men. That's what I ask—help, not worship!"

Tinglim rose slowly, as did the rest of the now-kneeling tribe. "Whatever you wish shall be. Come to our village. Be feasted, bathed, fed, as friends should be."

It sounded good.

Chapter 10

*Two hundred miles northwest of Rockson's party,
on the Al-Can Highway:*

Colonel Killov watched the snowy terrain move by
at a good clip from his warm and cozy cushioned
chair in the nose of his all-terrain vehicle. Equipped
with every convenience, the treaded trailer had been
built for General Dersky of Zhabnov's Supreme
Missile Command. But Dersky was no longer among
the living, and Killov had inherited the vehicle when
his troops captured Dersky's five truck-mounted
Megon-11 missiles in Idaho. Killov had lost four
hundred eighty-nine of his last seven hundred crack
Death's-head Commandos in that raid, but it had
been worth it.

Now he was headed north toward the Arctic Circle
with the five missiles on balloon-tired trucks behind
him. In another nine days—more or less—he would
be within firing distance of Moscow itself. And his
near rout in America, his failure to take over

99

America, would be reversed. Armed with the unstoppable Megon-11 cruise missiles that could fly eighty feet off the ground at twenty-eight hundred kilometers an hour, Vassily would have no choice but to surrender the Soviet World Empire to Killov's ironclad rule, or Moscow would be vaporized by the antimatter warheads of the missiles! If Vassily doubted that Killov would destroy Moscow, Killov would fire a missile toward Colorado, where he knew the American base called Century City was located. The entire west-central part of Colorado would be vaporized. That would show Vassily he meant business—and would also get Killov's nemesis, Ted Rockson, the "Doomsday Warrior," out of the way once and for all.

Killov had not yet been defeated! He smiled a cadaverous toothy grin, and popped an arunil pill into his lips and swallowed. In moments a flood of pleasure spread in his gut.

The well-equipped trailer he traveled in now was nothing compared to his living quarters on the top two floors of the Denver Monolith. His former headquarters, the eighty-story high, black, opaque Monolith dominated half the state. There he had a hundred servants, a command center that controlled hundreds of swift choppers and fifty thousand troops. Now the Monolith was besieged, soon to fall into the hands of the Red Army. But he would have it back, very soon.

They all thought he was beaten. But he wasn't yet. Repayment was about to be made. He would aim the missile just far enough away from Denver to have the mountains to the immediate west of the city shielded from total destruction. Of course Denver and half its million inhabitants would be shaken. Many would die. But the Monolith would stand. Then a few weeks later, his loyal troops—and defectors from the regular army hopefully, once they saw his power—would reoccupy his headquarters, restore *his* Capitol to its dark prominence.

Big plans. Plans that depended on no one knowing where he was for the next nine days, until Moscow was in his missiles' range.

Then let them know. Then let them kneel. It would be too late.

He took another pill, asyminol—a combination of several energy-stimulating drugs. He was a drug addict; his wasted skeletal body craved pills, not food. Killov hated to eat—even his vitamin-mix elixir was distasteful to his mega-drugged system. But the alarm on his watch/medical-alert instrument was beeping. He had to take sustenance. Resignedly, he opened a premixed vial of orange-colored vitamin fluid and drained it in a single swallow. Then in compensation he swallowed a megafetamine tablet.

Killov mused about his five missiles. Vassily had built the ultimate weapon—a force that used the destructive power of the universe, a contained "black hole" in time-space—and thus he had sealed his own doom. Killov broke into a big grin as the pill began leaking its aphrodisiac-hallucinatory stimulant into his intestines. His skeletal body quivered in ecstasy. He moved to the trailer's window to watch the snow go by. He hardly made it. Damned, he'd have to have more sustenance. The doctor that traveled with him at all times, Dr. Witowski, had set up an intravenous

101

feeding bottle and tube next to his airmatic bed-chair. Killov had a set of sterilized micro hypo needles in the drawer of the end table. He took one out now, attached it to the tube running from the hanging plastic bottle filled with bluish megavitamin and mineral protein glucose, and attached it to the tube. Then he jabbed the needle into the vein throbbing on his right forearm. It didn't hurt much, it never did, anymore. Still, there were so many scars on his arms that he'd soon have to start using his thighs.

He adjusted the flow meter and watched the enervating life-giving food in soluble solution drip-drip-drip down into the tube. It was infinitely better than chewing and swallowing.

Yes, I am sick, he thought, but I am *respected*.

They call me the skull, the monster, the dead man. So be it. Fear engenders respect. And respect engenders obedience. My troops will make this awesome journey through the coldest weather for me. No one would dare challenge me, or fates much worse than frozen death await them.

Killov picked up the interphone.

"How far north are we by the inertial readings, Mershneff?" he asked the driver of the vehicle.

"One hundred miles north of the forty-ninth parallel, Your Excellency," the driver stuttered out, checking the gauge on the immense, black, light-illuminated dashboard.

"And our speed?"

"Only thirty kilometers per hour, sir—the terrain is quite bumpy and cracked, and wind-blown drifts make it difficult for the ten half-tracks carrying the troops, and even for the missile trucks."

"Nevertheless, I want to reach the fifty-fourth parallel tonight. We've no time to dawdle. Notify all to move faster."

"Yes, Your Excellency. Immediately, Excellency."

The hum of the atomic-driven turbines went up a notch and Killov turned once again to the scene outside. He would be satisfied only when they reached the Yukon's mountains. Of course there would be a great danger there, for the land hadn't been explored since the nuke war over one hundred years earlier. But his crack troops, his equipment, would be up to it. And his protector, *Death Itself*, the all-powerful entropic power of the universe, had always protected Killov, for he was its most loyal servant.

Spirals of color began spinning in the snow outside as the numerous drugs in his body pushed him to the edge of hallucination. He had to lie down. He closed the window blinds. As he drifted in a drug-induced semitwilight, he thought, With Rockson dead I will have America, then the entire world, united under my absolute rule. Then I will destroy it. In a million atomic fires, end it all!

To be the *last* to live.

But first . . . Moscow had to surrender, then a brief atomic war of subjugation, nuking the rebel territories of Australia, South Asia, and the Micronesian Free States. Then, when the world is mine, he thought, from my space satellite station, I will press the button and blow everything, every living thing on the five-billion-year-old planet Earth away!

My master, Death, would be most happy . . .

103

Chapter 11

Rock saw wisps of smoke in the air, and when they crested a hill, there lay the Eskimo village. It was a group of several dozen igloos shimmering like immense half-pearls in the vast blanket of snow. Children played on small sleds pulled by husky pups. Women came out of the igloos, though, bundled as they were, it was hard to tell what sex they were. Only their softer complexions and long, silky black hair showed their gender.

Rock, and the Rock team—Archer, Chen, McCaughlin, and Detroit—plus Scheransky, were escorted to the largest white ice igloo.

"How the hell do you build these things anyway?" Rock asked curiously, as they approached the dome of ice.

"It must be done carefully," Tinglim said. "The entrance must not be in the direction of the prevailing west winds, but perpendicular to it. The igloos are just domes made of ice bricks; actually wind-snow. Highly compact and hard snow we cut

105

in the nearby drifts and cart here. They are laid upward in a spiral of diminishing diameter. If we had wood for scaffolds we would make bigger ones, but we migrate anyhow. So we abandon these igloos when the snowfall gets too heavy and buries them completely.

"Come, let us enter. Watch the ice steps, Rockson—they are steep and dark."

They passed through curtains and entered the open space inside—a pleasantly lit chamber hung with pelts. On a platform at the far end sat two Eskimo children in thick layers of clothing. They giggled upon seeing the strangers and crawled under the furs. In the middle of the room a small metal stove let its heat into the center but not the edges of the room. The walls were all glazed ice.

"A marvel of engineering," Scheransky said, "saves bricks too. Imagine, to make buildings out of frozen water!"

"Don't you know your own history?" Rock asked. "You Russians used to make huge palaces of ice during the Czar's winter carnivals, which were called *Moslenitza*. That was in the nineteenth century. Your Ivan the Terrible built an ice palace of clear ice on an island in the Volga River each winter. He made sure the walls were crystal clear on his side—he could see the ice castle from his own warm, heated palace. He filled the ice palace with naked virgins and horny dwarves. Ivan watched them try to keep warm together until they froze to death. Then he had his soldiers replace them with fresh victims. The sadistic pleasure of a diseased mind—right?"

Scheransky blushed. "I don't believe it—but if it is

true, that is one reason why we Communists had a revolution to overthrow the mad czars."

"But Soviet Russia still goes on torturing people all over the world," Rockson retorted heatedly.

Tinglim protested, "Stop! This is a peaceful house, no arguments! Come, let us sit on the bed platform. Because it is raised, it is the warmest place in the igloo. Let us have nice hot tea and discuss affairs of men, without women around." He clapped his hands together.

The Nara women withdrew after leaving teapots and cups.

It was warm. Rock and the others removed their ice boots at the edge of the platform and leaned against polar-bear-fur pillows and sipped the hot buttered tea.

"This is more like it," said Detroit. "But I don't understand how it can be, say, sixty degrees Fahrenheit here, and the ice wall doesn't melt."

"It is caused by currents of air from blow-holes," said Tinglim proudly, "Plus, of course, the force fields . . ."

"Force fields?" exclaimed Rock. "So that's the humming I thought I heard."

"Yes," Tinglim said. "The Ice City people gave us devices to generate force fields along the ice walls to prevent the warm and cold air from mixing. See the little boxes every five feet along the sides? Go over and touch a wall."

Rock did so, cautiously. There seemed to be some sort of almost magnetic resistance in the air which his hand had difficulty pushing through. Rockson returned to his seat.

"We could use some of these force field boxes," Rock said, thinking how Schecter would love to get his hands on one, dismantle it, and see what makes it tick.

After the tea, Rock and Tinglim sat alone by the small metal fireplace in the center of the igloo while the rest of the Rock Team explored other areas of the Eskimo encampment.

The Nara chief told the Doomsday Warrior legends of how his people experienced the Nuke War a hundred years earlier.

"My tribe saw the white lines in the sky, followed by the blossoming of orange glows in the south—in the United States and southern Canada. That glow was followed a few days later by terrible storms here, and then the falling of the 'burning rains.' There are tales from the old ones—who were children then—of mysterious sickness. Red boils on the skin, dryness of throat, a gradual withering away of the limbs. And then the birth of strange, mutated children—some more like fish than humans. The mutants were buried alive in the snows near the sacred mountains. Hunting was bad, and the village was starving by spring.

"All the land grew dry, withered, deserted. The lakes had no boats on them in the spring; the rivers and creeks had no canoes in them. No red-coated moose hunters came through our town asking for guides. It is told that one of our young men took a sleigh to find out what had happened. He set off to Nome, Alaska. When he came back, he was all sickly

108

and spotted. He died—but not before telling my people that instead of a white man's city, there was only a great circular ice lake, with the scattered burned bones of tens of thousands lining its shores.

"So my people stayed in this area. Our medicine men—we call them *Nyqwit*—told us not to wander, for the rest of the world had been poisoned by a Great Evil War.

"So," Tinglim continued, as Rock listened fascinated, "we stayed in this area and hunted as best we could and found leaves and berries to supplement our meager larders.

"My people were alone, cut off from the outside world, reduced to a few dozen families.

"Forsaking the old ways, and the *Nyqwit* advice, in a desperate search for food, we headed south, where the game was more plentiful. And came upon this unspoiled area. Here we thrived. Alone, for seventy or eighty years. Finally, others came. We have traded with other Eskimos and Indian tribes for the last thirty years. Our people grew so numerous that we split up—we the Nara Clan stayed in this area, near the ocean and fish. Others went into the forbidding Sasquatch Woods, and beyond it, built the Ice City."

"What's the Sasquatch Woods?" Rock asked.

"The Sasquatch, I believe, is what your people once called the 'Big Foot'—great hairy beasts with the strength of twenty men. Olmo may have been the offspring of human and Sasquatch parents. Although they have few weapons, except the huge rocks they throw—and they can throw enormous boulders—they have taken over all the land north of the Sasquatch River. They do not cross it, however. They

109

fear deep water. At this time of year, they usually hibernate in caves."

Rock could hardly believe all he was hearing, but he would soon find out. He decided that the Eskimos were great storytellers and that Tinglim was one of the best. But it was time for practical matters, not tall tales.

"I'm going to need supplies," Rock said, looking the Eskimo chief squarely in the eye.

"Whatever we have is yours—for a price," Tinglim replied, giving a coy look. The Nara leader took a long, slow sip of the hot buttered tea and then said, "I will sell you one sled with a husky team thrown in, for, say—one of your rifles and two hundred rounds of ammunition."

"I'll give you four rifles," Rock replied, "and a hundred rounds each, but I want eight sleds and dogs—one for each of my men. I'd like to leave here in eight hours."

"Ah," said Tinglim, "are you in a rush? If you are in a rush we can jack up the price. Are you in a big rush?"

Rock's mind raced for a second, "Well, not a *big* rush . . ."

"That's more like it," said Tinglim. "Tell you what. We send for your big arrow-shooting friend. He can bring some samples of your trading goods, particularly your skis-of-metal and your rifles, here. And I want to see some of your clever objects, like that compass you carry on your belt. Maybe I can make a counteroffer."

Tinglim slapped his hands together. A very pretty

Eskimo maiden, whom he introduced as Wiglim, came in with hot tea and some odd buns—lichen bread—on a tray. Tinglim instructed the girl to find Archer and tell him to bring all he could carry that might be a sample of what Rockson had to trade. Rock started to wish he had allowed Tinglim to consider him a god. It could become a costly mistake not to have done so.

In a matter of ten minutes, there was heavy breathing at the door, then the entrance shook. Archer came into the igloo carrying a vast mass of equipment: a giant armful that could have bent the chassis of a truck.

"Put if over there," frowned Rock. "Right by the door."

"Would your friend like some lichen buns?" asked Tinglim.

Rock's eyes rolled, "Would Archer like *food?* Does Lenin have a beard?"

Tinglim carefully inspected the Schecter skis, the compasses, sextants, knives, pistols, and camp gear Archer had brought in. "I take *all* this," he concluded, "And I give you four sleds and dog teams."

"No dice," Rock said.

This brought a pleased expression to the Eskimo's face. Out here men spent hours bartering—happy for the companionship.

"Very well, let us inspect your other goods."

The two of them walked outside to Rock's 'brid, Snorter. Rock unsheathed his new Liberator rifle from alongside the saddle. It was one of the newer

111

models that Rock had recently acquired from the arms factory.

Tinglim's fat brown hands ran covetously along the barrel of the perfectly machined 9mm rifle. He looked at the weapon closely, snapped the fifteen-round banana-clip in and out, admired the super-light magna-steel simulated-wood take-down stock. The weapon seemed to cause something approximating love in the man. He clicked the trigger, with the magazine out, of course, and then sighted along the barrel and gave an exclamation.

Tinglim had pointed it toward a husky, and had seen a tiny little red spot appear on the dog's fur.

"It's just the laser-locking mechanism," Rock said. "When you sight a target, the rifle shoots forth a harmless red laser beam. The beam leaves a trace of light-activated phosphorescence where it was focused. Then, if you pull the trigger and are off a bit, the bullets will skew to the right or left to find the target."

"Amazing," Tinglim muttered. "Amazing. Perhaps I could up my offer for some more sleds and dogs," Tinglim said, a greedy look in his eye. The Nara chief motioned to some men, said something in Naraese. Rock was then led back into the big igloo.

The Nara men brought in all kinds of artifacts, even jewels that Rock really didn't need, but couldn't resist looking at. The Doomsday Warrior nearly gasped out when he saw two neon-blue rabbitskin robes. They were beautiful, soft, and iridescent, catching every bit of light and reflecting it. Rock wanted them for Rona and Kim. The robes were of two sizes, one just right for each of the women.

"It took a hundred and fifty rabbits apiece to make them," Tinglim boasted. "And not ordinary rabbits. Neon rabbits. They have pelts that are dazzlingly blue, like the feathers of a peacock. "It takes great skill," said Tinglim, "to catch a neon rabbit. Then the pelts have to be dried and hung up in narrow strips. Then they are dressed and sewn together with walrus gut—very strong. Then they must be hung up in evergreen trees to catch the light of the aurora borealis, enhancing their color so that these robes are almost ultraviolet and glow. The coat that is made from them is light and warm. Wrapped in furs like that of the neon rabbit, a woman could walk in the coldest night without freezing."

Rock thought later that there might have been something in the tea to loosen up his mind. For he ended up trading quite a lot of supplies for the furs. Tinglim gave good value back, though, for another four rifles, some rounds, and compasses. He would board the 'brids while Rock traveled north, and promised to return the mounts, no strings attached, whenever the Freefighter came to claim them. They would be given foodstuffs for the trip, some of the harpoons the Eskimos used, a sled and six dogs for every member of the party, warm pelts, and a brick of Eskimo black tea, guaranteed to heat up the blood. Plus four clay gourds filled with highly volatile seal oil. "They might save your life—fuel to keep warm. Or to just make tea."

"Thanks for the tip," Rock said. But he began to wonder suddenly if his men had enough experience

113

in cold-weather survival to make the journey.

Almost as if reading his thoughts, Tinglim said softly, "You need me too, Rockson. I am coming along to help you—friend. We leave after a good rest for yourself and your men."

Rockson nodded and yawned. Some shut-eye was a good idea.

Chapter 12

An aged, frail man sat reading in his electric wheelchair on his "solarium," a glassed-in veranda overlooking Moscow. He was reading *On War*, by the Prussian military officer, Carl von Clausewitz. The book had been the basis of military strategy for the entire nineteenth century. He wrapped his shawl more closely about him as strontium-filled clouds passing over a wan sun cast chilling shadows over the city. Vassily, "the Grandfather," Premier of the world, gazed at the gray clouds that seemed to be threatening to envelop his empire. He'd just been reading of a campaign that had been won because the enemy had been blinded by the glare of the setting sun. That sort of strategy would never work now, he thought as the sun reemerged, resembling a shimmering stone in a pool of water.

Life must have been simpler then, Vassily thought. There were too many conflicting, constantly shifting forces in the world today. Not only were there rebellions in Afghanistan and China, but now even in the U.S.S.A. The Soviet forces were divided into two camps—the KGB Blackshirts versus his Red Army.

Vassily cursed himself for the hundredth time for leaving those missiles hidden in America. He cursed himself for not having disposed of Killov when he had the opportunity many years ago. His nephew, Zhabnov, though in general a fool, had repeatedly warned him that Killov was getting too powerful. Vassily had ignored him—putting it off to jealousy on Zhabnov's part. How could he have been so wrong? He was too old for all this. His life hung by the sheer slender thread of his willpower. But how long would the thread hold? One thing he vowed: he *must* last long enough to see Killov destroyed. Then he would gladly sink into the abyss.

Rahallah, Vassily's black manservant, appeared at the doorway carrying a red phone. The Premier looked up at the descendant of African kings and wondered what he would ever do without him. The strength emanating from Rahallah's sculpted face with its high cheekbones was more than physical—it was character. The kind of character that had made him Vassily's most trusted aide and adviser. "The operator has finally reached Washington," Rahallah said quietly as he placed the phone on a little table beside Vassily. The Premier of all the earth nodded as he placed his book in his lap and pushed the little button that activated the phone.

President Zhabnov was handed a steaming cup of

demitasse by Gudonov. He leaned back in the restored and enlarged JFK rocking chair, which had somehow survived the KGB invasion, and took a relaxing sip. The low winter sunlight was streaming pleasantly through the Oval Office's casement windows. This was more like it. He felt fully relaxed for the first time since he'd arrived back in Washington.

Suddenly the red phone rang. *Vassily.* It was *Vassily!* Zhabnov's trembling fingers put down the cup. Gudonov brought the phone over and handed him the receiver. Zhabnov, sitting at attention, placed it to his ear. "Hello?"

"This is the Premier, Nephew. How are you?"

Zhabnov replied, "Just fine, Uncle. You should have seen the trememdous welcome I received here. The people love me; they showered me with flowers . . ." he lied.

"Yes, yes, Nephew. I know it must be gratifying to receive such a welcome. I am sure everyone is glad that you are back." Vassily said—the tone of his voice revealing he didn't believe his nephew for a second. "Have you read the orders I placed in your briefcase before you left Moscow?"

Zhabnov paled. What orders? His mind groped for words.

"Oh, *those.* Of course I read them," Zhabnov lied, wondering what could be so important in them. Bureaucratic things, no doubt.

"Well, what have you done to implement them?" Vassily asked with growing impatience.

What in Stalin's moldy face was he talking about,

117

Zhabnov thought anxiously. "Why, everything possible . . . under the circumstances," he answered hesitantly.

"What circumstances?"

"The White House is a shambles. Leaks are everywhere. We're operating with a skeleton staff . . . and, and my rose garden is ruined and—"

"Stop whining, you fool. This is a matter of extreme importance. Intelligence has reached us that there may be KGB agents left in your area. They must be wiped out. You must reestablish your leadership over your scattered army—before there is a counterattack."

"But Uncle, Killov is dead! He died when Rockson blew up the Octagon prison."

"Nephew, you are forever misinformed. Killov lives and has stolen five Megon missiles. He is now somewhere in Canada."

"Tell me but where, Your Excellency, and I will instantly destroy him."

"Fool. I'm already taking care of the matter. I don't need your inefficiency to gum up the works."

Zhabnov turned red, and after a pause, to control his blood pressure said, "I am sure, Uncle, that you will handle the matter *most* efficiently. But if I could be of any assistance . . ."

"I will let you know. But you will be of most assistance to me and yourself if you rally your troops, if you secure the eastern United States once more, round up the fragments of KGB traitors that still exist. Get your house in order, Nephew, before it crumbles around your head.

"If this is beyond you," Vassily continued, "I can

replace you with a smarter man . . . Rahallah, for example?"

"That witch doctor!"

"Ah, Nephew. It would be wise to watch your tongue. Rahallah is my invaluable assistant and adviser."

"Yes, Your Excellency," Zhabnov answered resignedly. He heard the *click* as Vassily hung up the receiver.

Zhabnov groaned. "There must be a way . . ." he muttered.

General Barishkov sat panting in a storm drain on the outskirts of Washington, D.C. He'd been on the run ever since Zhabnov, commander-in-chief of the U.S.S.A. Red Army, had announced on TV that he wished to meet his officers at the Capitol Building the next day. Rain mixed with sweat fell off his brow. God! it's cramped in here, he thought. Meet! That's a good one. Barishkov would be stripped of his rank and thrown in the brig. Spetsnaz Commandos in their green uniforms were probably arresting generals all over the city. He'd be lucky if he got demoted to private. He deserved to be shot for skulking away when the going got rough. He knew it. He felt ashamed. He never even knew what hit him. He had been taking R&R on the Silver Bullet when it was commandeered by the Freefighters. When he'd begged for mercy, he was forced to strip to his underwear and then squeezed with two officers into a reinforced nylon mail bag. He and two others had been left swinging on a hook of the train line's mail service somewhere in Indiana.

That would have been hard enough to live down. But when his troops were defeated at the Washington train station by KGB Blackshirts, he'd snuck away, hiding for his life. He'd kept secreted in his apartment—until he heard the knock on his door, then he'd slid down the rope to the alley and then here.

He glanced out the entrance to the storm drain. Barishkov thought he'd heard a noise—perhaps a cat? No, he heard martial footsteps outside the drainpipe.

He made a run for it to the other side of the culvert—but *too late*. There were two guards on the other end of the tunnel. It was no use to resist. He crawled out, his arms waiting for the bullets to tear into his flesh. One of the Spetsnaz troopers motioned with his automatic. Barishkov walked between the two guards until he was roughly shoved into the sidecar of a motorcycle. "Got another one," said the guard ominously. "It's getting late. Better take him directly to the Capitol Building."

"Yes, *sir*," saluted the driver. As the motorcycle shot off leaving a burning trail of rubber behind, Barishkov bounced in his seat. He stared at the leather-jacketed driver as the bike sped through the city streets. They sped up Pennsylvania Avenue past the Grant Memorial to the Capitol Building front steps.

"Get out," the driver said. Barishkov slowly stepped out of the sidecar and noticed that a half-dozen other generals were being dragged, kicking and screaming, into the building. He had more pride left than that, he thought. He walked up the step between guards like a man. He'd die on his feet, not begging on his knees.

When they reached the rotunda, Barishkov's heart skipped a beat. It was decorated with streamers. Banquet tables had been set up laden with food. Elaborate food, at that. A band was playing on a bandstand. Zhabnov's got a macabre sense of humor, thought Barishkov. He's going to make a party out of stripping stars off us. The bandleader struck his baton on the podium. "Pomp and Circumstance" was played. Zhabnov, resplendent in medals, stepped out to the podium.

"Gentlemen, please be seated," he said as soon as the music stopped. The crowd settled down into their seats. Zhabnov cleared his throat. Several nervous coughs could be heard throughout the rotunda. He stroked his greasy wisp of a beard. Suspense built as he looked around with a fat smile plastered on his jowled face.

"As you know, I've had you brought here for a purpose." He bided his time, letting his words take effect. Several officers squirmed in their seats. Some pulled at their tight collars or fidgeted with their neckties. "I wanted you to know how I feel about your performance during the recent sieges of Washington. . . . I'm going to . . ." The generals braced themselves. "I'm going to give you all medals and special privileges, and raise your salaries," finished Zhabnov.

An audible gasp filled the rotunda. After a few moments of silence, one of the generals began to clap. Then another. Soon the entire assembly of officers were clapping their hands. A roar of approval and relief spread through the crowd. Zhabnov held his hands up for silence. He took a medal off a green felt table near him and called out the first name. General Barishkov. General Barishkov walked to the podium. He could hardly believe this. Was it a dream?

"For your feats of bravery at the Washington train station, I award you with the Distinguished Medal of Valor."

General Barishkov was speechless as Zhabnov pinned the medal on his chest and then saluted him. "You really ought to have your suit pressed," Zhabnov whispered. Barishkov returned the salute and went back to his seat.

When the medal awarding was over, Zhabnov clapped his hands. A servant pulled back a purple curtain and several dozen beautiful slender American women in evening gowns entered the room. The band started to play a waltz and soon everyone was dancing and drinking—from imminent death to hedonistic bliss in minutes.

A successful party, thought Zhabnov as he drove away from the Capitol Building in the back seat of his Zil limo, toward the White House. *That* should take care of it, he thought. The officers are back in my corner. Grateful for their very lives. They will get their men back in order, destroy the remnants of the KGB.

Chapter 13

Under Tinglim's close supervision, the quiet Eskimo community turned into a bustling beehive of activity. Men were put to work preparing hunting equipment. The women were sewing warm sealskin clothes big enough for Rockson and his men. The rest of the village was occupied gathering the necessary items: portable stoves, fuel, blankets, tents, quantities of meat—narwhal, walrus, caribou, seal, and lesser game—that had already been accumulated in the Eskimo camp for the long winter. All were brought to the trading igloo to be loaded on the sleds. The sleds chosen were the lightest and strongest in order to maintain the greatest speed to catch up with Killov. The huskies were the most reliable and well-trained.

Rockson stepped out of the comfortable igloo into the bitter-cold, but clear, outside world. He flipped down his slit snowglasses to prevent snow blindness and put up his fur-lined parka hood. The sleds, which were always turned sideways off their runners when not in use, were set upright ready to be loaded. The huskies were ready to be harnessed to them—six dogs to a sled, hitched up much the way a team would be hitched to a wagon. Tinglim and Rock walked around inspecting each dog. They were fine creatures, furry healthy huskies—not-so-distant relatives to the wolves that stalked the snow-wrapped hills. Each weighed about eighty pounds and had footpads of coarse black skin that tracked snow with surprising grip. Their ears perked up the minute anyone walked over to them, and they seemed to enjoy when they were petted. Rock also noted that they had pretty good canine teeth—they were meat eaters and didn't care what sort of meat it was. He filed that away for future reference—just in case.

"This here's Niqytl, the biggest of the dogs," Tinglim said, as he hitched the lead dog to the team of Rockson's red sled. "I think you will want him because he is such a good leader and responds well to the whip."

In short order everything was made ready. Rockson and his men—Chen, Archer, Detroit, McCaughlin, Scheransky, Robinson, Pedersen, and Farrell helped load the sleds and harness the dogs. Nine sleds were loaded with two hundred pounds each of expedition supplies. The tenth sled carried the antimatter detector, which Scheransky would continue to monitor from time to time to keep them on Killov's trail.

The 'brids, unbridled and corraled to the south of the Eskimo village, were given some evergreen branches to chew by their attendant, a young boy. Rockson said a special "So long but not good-bye," to Snorter. "I'll be back for you, old pal." He handed the 'brid a piece of candy that he had secreted in his pocket. Snorter whinnied in joy and took it. Rock patted him on the forehead and went back to the dog sleds.

The dim sun went behind a hill. The day was ending long before it really began; the sun would be down for twenty hours. In the dimness, everything looked ghostly: the moundlike igloos, the slit eyes of the villagers watching the preparations, even the dogs seemed to glow in the half-light.

Some villagers lit torches to make the trek's preparation area more visible to them.

Tinglim said to Rock, "You know, I am glad you have come to us. It is time for adventure." He smiled. "That is the Eskimo way. It is fitting for men to go far and risk death!"

As the expedition party were putting on their skis one of Tinglim's wives hurried out of the igloo carrying a tin. "Don't forget tea!" she said emphatically. The Eskimo husband took the tin from his wife and rubbed noses with her. "Take care of Tinglim for me," she said to the Doomsday Warrior.

"I will," Rockson replied. But he knew he was the one who'd have to rely on Tinglim and his special knowledge. Rockson had to trust Tinglim's choice of food, for one thing. Tinglim knew what wild plants and lichens were edible and how to stalk the northern animals. They had to rely on game to feed the dogs and themselves on route. The Eskimo knew how to build an emergency igloo and a hundred other different ways to survive in this arctic wasteland. Most of all, Tinglim could navigate in this uncharted wilderness when compass and sextant failed, and could find the fastest and safest route over difficult terrain. But he was a strong-willed man, unused to taking orders. This could pose a threat, Rockson knew, to his command.

There were three ways to run such an expedition. One was to be an absolute dictator and decide everything for the others. Its opposite was to vote on everything. But a dictatorship would invite revolt and total democracy got too unwieldy in times of extreme danger. Rockson would have to steer a fine line between the two—ask opinions and then make the final decision. But there could be only *one* leader. He had to find a way to show Tinglim who was boss at the outset without seeming to do so. In a few moments, the opportunity arose to solve the matter.

Tinglim said loudly, "We must all stow our skis and ride with our feet on the skid-ends of the sleds."

"But that weighs down the sleds," Rockson objected. "We must move fast, Tinglim. We have to wear the short skis and glide behind the sleds holding on. It would take some weight off the dogs."

"It *won't* work," answered Tinglim, "because our feet will get cold from the transference of temperature from the snow under the skis. Also, the skis tend to get fouled up in the sleds. I know this from experience."

"But these are special skis," replied Rockson. "They're not only shorter than regular skis, but they're made with an insulating alloy. Care to put them to the test?" challenged Rockson. "Your method against mine? We race a mile or so with the sleds. Okay?"

Tinglim couldn't refuse such a challenge. He figured that with his years of experience driving the dogs, it was a cinch to win. "Okay. We race from this igloo to that hill over there and back. It's about two miles round trip." Before the men could prepare their respective sleds, word had passed through the entire village.

Chen cut a starting line on the packed snow and made sure that both contestants lead dogs were right on the mark.

The excitement in the air was catching and the dogs strained against their reins. Rockson wished he'd had more time to learn how to run the dog sleds. He didn't have time to worry, because suddenly Idluk, a man from the village, gave the starting shot—and they were off.

Both men shouted and cracked their whips. Tinglim's lead dog leaped into the effort. The Eskimo crowd roared. Rockson cracked his whip, too far over the dogs to make them move. But he remembered Tinglim's advice: It's all in the wrist . . . Soon he hit the mark just inches over their ears. As his team headed down the slope from the village, Rockson began to gain speed, catching up to Tinglim's early lead. Shortly thereafter, they were hidden from view by the night. Rockson's men and the Eskimos placed bets with each other as to who would win. Detroit took down the bets. "I'll bet five 9mm bullets on Rockson," McCaughlin said heartily.

"I'll match that bet and raise you ten that Tinglim wins," retorted Idluk, Tinglim's stocky cousin.

"Put me down for Rockson winning by two sled

lengths," yelled Chet Robinson, stroking his red beard for good luck.

"We bet a bottle of seal wine that Tinglim wins by four lengths," said the two Eskimo dog handlers, "versus ten 9mm bullets. Okay?"

"Done," said Robinson, peering into the distance.

Detroit was surrounded by a pushing, shoving if friendly crowd yelling out their winner and holding bullets or goods in their upraised hands trying frantically to place their bets before the race was over. After ten minutes, someone's voice screamed, "They're coming back!" All betting ceased. They strained their eyes to take in the winner. "I see them," someone yelled. "It's Rockson." Yes, Rockson was in the lead, his team moving like a racing machine. However, under the whip, Tinglim's lead dog, Balto, was not to be outdone. Tinglim's team pulled inches ahead. Then it was Rockson, then Tinglim. "It might be close," Detroit yelled.

Idluk and Chen got on opposite sides of the finish line in case it was a photo finish, but Rockson and his team won by a length. It was a decisive victory for Rockson's leadership. While Detroit was deciding who got what as far as the bets were concerned, Tinglim and Rockson put down their sleds and moved off to the side, out of the light of the orange-flamed torches.

Tinglim eyed Rockson appraisingly before he spoke. His eyes caught the glow of the orange flames. "You were right about the skis," Tinglim admitted. "With my experience, I should have won. When this trek is over, I'd like to race you again—this time I too will wear short skis."

"Ah, but you forget," answered Rockson. "By then I, too, will be experienced, and you'll still lose."

At that a twinkle came to Tinglim's eye, then both laughed. The tension was broken. And Rockson knew that from this time on, he'd have no trouble with his command.

Detroit, having completed the divvying up of the winnings, skiied over to join Rockson and Tinglim. He looked disappointed.

"What's the matter?" asked Rockson. "You didn't bet against me, did you?"

"I got so busy taking bets that I forgot to place one myself," Detroit groaned.

"I've got something to cheer you up," said McCaughlin coming up behind Detroit. He displayed one of his winnings—a large bottle of Mugatawny brandy. "I propose a drink for all," McCaughlin said cheerily. "Here's to snow."

It was time to go!

Rock told Tinglim to take the lead. Rockson's sled followed Tinglim. Scheransky was next. He had charge of the sled with the antimatter detector. Robinson brought up the rear.

"*Mush, mush, you huskies,*" Tinglim yelled, snapping the whip over his team. The dogs surged forward.

The sleds crept forward, then, meeting little resistance to the snow, leapt forward. Chen managed to grab hold of the trail handles and slide along behind his sled on his steel skis. "It sure beats the hell out of traveling by 'brid," he yelled to Detroit when the black Freefighter caught up and pulled alongside. "But hang on tight!"

It was phenomenally clear. Galaxies of stars could be seen and the moon shone down like a guiding beacon. It would be many hours yet before a belt of orange on the southeast horizon heralded the barely rising sun. It was a cold minus-twenty-six degrees Fahrenheit. But all were rested and well dressed. The sleds on the unbeaten track swayed and whispered over the snow. From the front of the snow parade came Tinglim's low, hoarse voice grunting at his dogs. Every now and then one of the dogs would let out a howl like a wolf, sending shivers down the spines of Rock and his crew.

The run began with enthusiasm. The men laughed and joked. Archer played around so hard he almost lost control of his sled. But the good spirits died down after a few hours. It had grown windier and the effort of talking had become too much. Besides, the warm air of their breath had a tendency to condense on their faces and turn to ice.

Mile after mile, Rockson kept his mutant senses on full alert. He could see Tinglim's sled to the front of him over the trails of his own dogs. His feet were beginning to feel numb, but it wasn't only the wind and cold that took his breath away. It was the awesome beauty of the northern landscape. Miles of snow in every direction looked like oceans or deserts turning purple, now pink, then orange, and finally gold with the glow reflected from the northern lights above. Snow hares could be seen sitting with their ears pricked alert, sitting motionless on the hills. Once he saw a caribou raise its regal antlered head to gaze at them briefly before returning to feed on lichens hidden by the snow. In the distance he could

130

see some dark shapes. Mountains, indistinct, hard to make out. Clouds had appeared in the night with the growing light of the aurora's multicolored shifting curtain behind them, and began to cast drifting shadows.

Tinglim had told Rock that Eskimos had a belief concerning shadows. They believed that man's soul is separate from the body and that it resides in his shadow. Stormy or lightless days are gloomy to Eskimos because the shadow is not in evidence. The soul has departed and may not return. Rockson had never thought about it before . . . For an Eskimo, the joy of seeing his shadow once again is intoxicating. But for Rockson, shadows meant something else—danger, something that went by night, something unseen but seeing. It was fitting that Killov should escape to hide in the dark of the Arctic's long night. To crawl into the six-month-long shadow of the earth. What dark thoughts lurked behind the bony mask? What threat for humanity?

"Let me live," the Doomsday Warrior prayed, "—at least until I've finished off Killov—before he destroys the living world and brings on the night forever, a darkness with no shadows and no light."

Suddenly Tinglim picked up speed. He was going faster and faster. It was all Rockson and his men could do to keep up with the Nara. It seemed as if they were on a runway and were about to take off—when just as suddenly the Eskimo slowed and stopped. The other sleds almost jammed into each other.

"What is it?" asked Rock, somewhat alarmed.

"It's time for tea," answered Tinglim. "The dogs need a rest."

"So do we," said Detroit. The men were encouraged to take off their skis and stamp their feet to get their circulation going again. Within minutes the tea was ready, heated on the porta-stove. They sat around the heat on pelts.

"Boy, that's good," said Chen. The warmth of the tea coursed through their veins, loosening their tongues stiff from the cold. A tale was spun by Tinglim, about the birth of the world from a seal spat up by a polar bear. The Freefighters listened with broad smiles at the drawn-out myth as they sipped from steaming cups. Above, the northern lights burned as if the very sky was on fire.

Rockson noticed with unease that one of the auroral curtains seemed to shape itself like a bony hand and close. Then it was gone.

Chapter 14

Colonel Killov tossed and turned in his sleep, a cold sweat beading on his forehead. Rockson, his dreaded enemy, Rockson, coming at him with a huge knife, holding a box in the other hand. There was something about the box—its size . . .

The dream. Killov asked, "What is the box for?" He tried to move but was frozen in place. Other figures, other Americans, moved in around the bed and started laughing. Echoing laughter. Rockson stepped forward, his face bending and twisting in a grin.

"Killov, I am removing your head. Putting it in this box. It will be in a museum. You will be famous. You want that, don't you?"

Killov tried to say "*No*—no—no—no . . ."

He fell out of bed. His heart was pounding. He gasped for air. Not real. Only a dream. Not real.

When he was a little calmer he sat at his desk and wondered about the nightmare. Maybe it's a warning from the Dark One. Maybe Rockson is close—on my trail. What can I do? Send someone behind me—a whole platoon? No, I need the men, it could be a false warning propelled on by this awful near-endless night of the Arctic. But I need someone strong . . . Who?

Chrome. Of course. The metal man. The killing machine who had single-handedly disposed of ten guards at the Idaho missile base from which the missiles were taken. He was the one. He owed Killov something. His life. The life Rockson had taken from him. The life Killov's scientists had brilliantly restored. An experiment in cyborg creation that had partially succeeded. Chrome was too dangerous, too unpredictable to have along anymore. Chrome was so menacing, so fearful looking, that even Killov was afraid to see him alone. For the man had no real features or head for that matter. He had been an SS Commando in Von Reisling's Nazi army, and when Von Reisling had died, the special Commando had become Killov's to command—if he could. Killov had used him well, pitting Chrome against many. His face had been blown off by an American rocket in the battle of Forester Valley. An experimental operation had been performed.' An operation that put together the mutilated pieces of Commando Gunter, to create Chrome. Science had fashioned a new face and skull out of chrome steel, shiny and impenetrable, to encase his brain and mouth and throat. He didn't talk much, but he still took orders. For now.

Killov sat there on the edge of his bed for a long time, feeling the gentle roll of the trailer over the ice and snow before he decided: Chrome would be a one-man patrol a hundred miles behind. He'd be given enough food and ammo to keep alive, if he could hunt up a meal now and then. The other soldiers didn't like him around anyway. He was a born killer devoid of any comradely instincts. He would sit perfectly still and just watch them all play cards or talk, his unblinking reconstructed eyes following any movement around the area.

It would be a morale booster to be rid of him. Killov ordered his aide to bring Chrome to him.

A half-hour later, the metal man stood before Killov's desk.

"Chrome," said Killov through his thin lips, "your mission is to drop back behind us and intercept and destroy any pursuers. I don't *expect* any pursuers but I've learned to never underestimate the Freefighters. You are to plant booby traps, mines. I suggest that there are several places behind us—unstable rock formations, glacial buildups—that could be rigged with small explosive charges. They should be set to go off if someone passes below."

Chrome's lips of metal parted, and a vibrating tone that sounded more like an icy computer than a man said, "It will be done. I have longed for the opportunity to leave the emotional rabble you call your troops behind. They complain and worry. I do neither. It is my pleasure to seek out the enemies of the Soviet State, for you, Killov. The World Soviet must not be ruled by weaklings. I have anticipated your order and have modified the Dragunov-II sniper rifle for greater power. I will carry that and the explosives with me. I will range far and wide behind you, seeking out and destroying any who follow. As

135

you know, I am impervious to cold. I will function. When shall I return?"

Killov feared this metal man. And he was sure he said the right thing when he replied, "Never. Never return. Keep seeking out those who would oppose me. Keep heading south, into the United States itself, if you do not find my enemies at my heels. I order you to do this for I believe in your power. Fulfill your destiny—*kill*."

The metal face stared impassively for a moment at Killov. Although the KGB leader had had a pistol loaded with special high-explosive bullets trained on the metal man from beneath his desk for the entire interview, Killov wondered if the bullets would be enough, should he not like his orders.

Chrome, his impassive chrome-steel head not showing any emotion, said, "I accept the order of my superior."

Equipment was prepared for him and with his long-range Dragunov sniper rifle and infrared scope, explosives, climbing rope, and skis, he was sent off.

Killov was relieved when he was gone. He didn't like the way the man's yellow synthsteel eyes stared at him, nor the way his hands kept clenching in immense steel fists.

Let someone follow me now, the KGB commander thought. Let them come up upon Chrome and try to reason with the metal-faced stranger. Let them plead with him. Killov laughed. And then he started coughing. He popped a few arthoval pills and fell back in his recliner. He shouted out an order for the caravan to resume its pace forward toward the Arctic Circle.

Chapter 15

Tinglim passed Rockson the steaming cup of Eskimo tea. They were cold, but thawing out, sitting Indian-style around the small fire made from dry lichen. Tinglim's crude map was on his lap.

"That mountain is called Mount Draco," Tinglim said pointing to a single upside-down V that was burned into the seal-pelt map.

"The X is my village," he explained, putting his wide forefinger on the lower left corner. "So we've made good time. Judging from our speed, and the number of hours we've traveled, we're about here," he said, tracing the finger directly north from the X to a spot one third of the way to Mount Draco and near a long, snaking line.

"What river is that?" asked Rockson, beginning to get the hang of the crude map.

"That's the Draco River. It flows directly from Mount Draco's glacier which is approximately *there*," said Tinglim, pointing to a line drawn along the river's bank at its north end. "*There* is the danger."

"What do you mean?"

"Well, periodically the glacier surges, advancing without warning. When a glacier decides to move, it moves. The last time it surged, it crossed the Draco River valley and blocked the river, forming a lake. The next time it surges, it could wash out the ice dam. The resulting floods would be awesome."

"Why can't we cross the glacier itself?—above the breaking point."

"Because the hills would be too steep for the dogs. Just below the breaking point a surge shattered the ice into a hellish landscape. It would be like ants trying to cross the Himalayas. We'd never get the sleds and dogs across. The way directly north is blocked by the highest mountains in the Yukon Range. Our only hope is to follow the river, which should be frozen solid.

"Once across, we'll be about a day's journey from the Sasquatch Forest," he said, pointing to a group of triangles designating trees etched into the map. "Beyond that is Ice City," the Nara chief finished, pointing to the X beyond the trees.

"The area beyond the forest, on the other side of Ice City, is blank because I don't know what is there," Tinglim said, shrugging his shoulders. "But there is a legend that evil spirits guard the place and that it is a no-man's land from which none returns." Tinglim rolled up the pelt.

Rockson could see that there would be no further discussion regarding the blank area, and let the matter drop. As they both stood up and started to walk back to their sleds Rockson asked, "You *did* say the Sasquatch would be hibernating, right?"

"I don't think we'll have to worry about them. They usually begin hibernation about this time. But I can't *guarantee* that. The aurora seems to enrage them, and keeps them awake, and there's been a lot of it, as you have seen lately.

"Yes," Rockson replied, "But that same aurora will help us see our way when the moon is below the horizon."

"One more thing," added Tinglim, putting on his skis. "I didn't want to tell you before, but now I have to. If the Draco River is frozen solid, we can just sail across. But there are geysers of hot water underneath that are just as unpredictable as the glacial surges. It can cause monstrous crevasses, or thin ice areas. From now on you will have to pay close attention to the surface ice when we ride. The crevasses can come up very suddenly. It is not something that should be approached in darkness," Tinglim added ominously.

A blanket of snow was beginning to fall as the party remounted their sleds. A cold wind from the Arctic north blew right in their faces as the dogs started forward once again. The soft powdery substance accumulated quickly, making the sleds drag, impeding the movement of the dogs. Rock knew that this was only the beginning of things to come. Further north the weather would be even more fickle. This flurry could become a blizzard, and with a constant wind could make snow drifts high enough to bury them forever.

The outline of the mountain grew larger. Low-slung clouds masked its full height with tendrils of wispy fog. Then Mount Draco's peak became visible above the twisting veils. It was as if the mountain was a thing alive. Breathing. That mountain was going to try to take a life. Rock was sure of it.

The wind picked up and seemed to penetrate Rockson's bones despite the warm clothing. The snow made it ever more difficult to make out Tinglim's sled over the tails of his dogs. The brief "day" dawned for an hour and then was gone.

The sky turned pink and then purple.

The snow blinded Rockson, stinging his face. It seemed to penetrate even the superfine stitching of his gear and attack him. It grew more difficult to breathe the icy air. Rock momentarily looked back to see how the other sleds were doing, but he could see no further than about fifteen feet behind him. And when he turned his head forward Tinglim had vanished into the wall of white. Rockson strained his eyes to find the Nara but he had disappeared in the blinding snow. Rock barely made out something lying directly in his path—it was like a lake of pure black. He was within feet of it when he realized with horror what it was. The Doomsday Warrior swung sharply away in an instant and brought his sled up into the wind. He yelled, *"STOP!"* at the top of his lungs, hoping that the men were near. He was standing on the edge of a chasm—he was within inches of a yawing black, bottomless abyss. The chasm was broad enough and deep enough to comfortably swallow the entire expeditionary force and have plenty of room for more.

"Thank God," Tinglim said from behind his left shoulder. Rock jumped, startled to see the Eskimo. He'd thought for a moment that Tinglim had been the trek's first victim.

"My damned lead dog went after something to the right. It only took a second to separate me from the rest of you," Tinglim said. "Up here, disaster, death, is always just a second away. We must now proceed with utmost caution," Tinglim went on. "Where there is one crevasse are others. It is imperative that each of you follow in single file, directly in my tracks."

Tinglim started skiing parallel to the crevasse in front of his sled. Using a staff he kept poking through the snow to see if there was solid ground underfoot. The dogs perked up their ears and took care that each paw hit solid ground. But fearing the loss of a dog, they were unharnessed. Humans became the muscle power to move the vehicles. The dogs, reined together, trailed, watching. After a mile or so the miserably cold men came to the end of the crevasse and could continue on their way. But then they came upon a veritable field of smaller cracks, many hidden under the most recent snow. A jammed skid could destroy a sled. But the loads were toward the middle of the sleds. Again and again, they were able to tip the front end of a sled up in the air until it was once again over solid ground; as the sled spanned the crack, the driver would leap across the crevasse and pull it on. This all made tough work—yards felt like miles. At times there were comparatively long distances between cracks, and the men wanted to take a breather, but Rockson pushed them on, reminding

141

them that there was very little time left. They'd have to take advantage of every day of endurable weather.

The temperature dropped to minus thirty degrees Fahrenheit—made even colder by the lack of sun and by the howling wind. The field of cracks ended finally. The dogs were rehitched, none lost. But then came another obstacle to defeat. Snow, driven against scattered boulders began to form into drifts around them, making the going even tougher than before. The wind drove the snow like a hurricane of knife blades into their faces, cutting the skin, the blood freezing as it oozed out. Their nostrils seemed glued together by the cold, making breathing almost impossible. Robinson's red beard was now covered with ice. Archer looked like he had a bib of cotton. Their feet began growing numb, and their hands frostbitten—despite the caribou-hide mittens. Secretly each man half hoped that Rockson would tell them to turn back, or at least tell them to camp down for the storm. Then they would crawl exhausted into their tents and into their fur sleeping pallets. At least to find shelter from the wind.

At last the Doomsday Warrior's hand went up and he told them to stop. He tested a large area with his spiked ski pole and found it safe.

"We'll make camp here."

The howling snowstorm was now a full-fledged blizzard. Rockson knew that it would be impossible to go on now—or even to pitch tents in this wind.

He approached Tinglim. "How long does a blow like this last?" he shouted.

Tinglim yelled, "A day. Maybe two. It is imperative to construct a shelter. We must begin by digging a pit."

Rock thought the idea impossible, but he knew he had to rely on Tinglim's judgment. He didn't know what the hell else to do. He gave the order to dig. All hands removed the shovels from the sleds, gathered in one corner of the snowbank, and began to dig. The snow was piling up almost faster than they could shovel. Still, they kept shoveling. Within half an hour four of the men could fit inside. It took another half-hour for the rest. Tinglim directed the piling up of snow blocks cut with knives to be passed upward from the interior. The wind raged on like a madman. The dogs huddled together like a single ball of fur in the snow to keep from freezing. Somehow the men built a crude but functional igloo.

Inside they could even remove their parkas. Tinglim lit a whale-oil heater. The emergency igloo was filled with the fragrance of unwashed men and dried blubber which the Nara chewed happily. Two lamps were used to melt water out of snow and ice. McCaughlin set up the stove. Soon a coffee smell permeated the air. Everyone congratulated Tinglim: Let the winds howl outside. They were warm.

"Is there actually dinner?" Rock asked McCaughlin, who was rapidly setting up the small cookstove.

"I'm cooking already," McCaughlin answered. "Rabbit legs in pea soup. Ersatz coffee will be ready in a few minutes, as soon as the ice has melted and boiled!"

"They spent the night in something less than luxury surroundings—but their stomachs were full and they weren't freezing to death.

It was twenty-four hours before they could again

143

venture out. The blizzard at last moved on, leaving behind it a starry moonlit sky and warmer temperatures—all the way up to zero degrees. The party set off again, making excellent speed. After seven hours they were at the Draco River which was frozen solid. They started making their way up it, as the ice was a good six inches thick.

They sped along like they were being pursued by the devil himself, not quite positive the ice river was going to hold them up, and wanting to get off it as soon as possible. The river at this position headed nearly directly north, parallel to the Al-Can Highway, and they were making up precious time, moving thirty or forty miles along in a matter of hours. Suddenly there was a yelping and howling from the lead dogs of Rockson's sled and they skidded to a halt, the other dogs tripping and bumping into one another.

The two dogs at the head of Rock's sled sunk in to their haunches through cracked ice. Steam rose. They howled as their paws hit the near-boiling temperature of the waters under the ice—an underground hot spring had melted the ice cover to the thickness of a pane of glass. They splashed about vainly trying to get out of the deathtrap, but couldn't get their footing. Rockson gingerly stepped from the sled—even this small movement caused cracks to appear under his boots—and he looked down and saw rushing blue waters just inches under his own feet.

"Take to the ground," Rockson yelled to the other men. But they were already doing that—the sleds behind being driven toward the safety of the snowy banks.

"Throw ropes to Rockson from the rear and help pull the lead dogs out of the water," the Nara chief shouted as he pulled back to a safe distance and brought his team to a stop.

Rockson saw the two lead dogs going deeper. He heard a cracking and a hissing as a lower layer of the ice cracked and buckled all around him. His slightest movement caused more cracks to open.

The huskies were treading near-boiling water, not supported at all by the ice.

The whole team of dogs let out mournful howls, knowing they soon would also be in the steaming waters.

A rope flew toward Rockson. He saw it out of the corner of his eye and grabbed it, just snagging the end. He tied it to the handle of the sled and secured it. Then another rope flew over his shoulder. He did the same with that just as the sled began slipping forward again. Within seconds the second set of dogs broke through the ice, and then the final two dogs went in as well.

"Pull, you bastards, pull," McCaughlin and Chen screamed at their teams. Each Freefighter had managed to get a rope to Rockson from opposite sides of the frozen river of death. Their dogs slipped and scurried for traction, feeling the strain of the weight of Rockson's sinking sled.

Rockson was about ready to abandon everything— the supplies *and* the dogs—to their watery grave. He was inches deep in the bubbly hot water already, his feet soaking wet, nearly scalded inside the boots. He figured if he worked his way along one of the ropes, slid himself along the still-frozen ice, he might make it—alone. Suddenly the sled stopped its plunge and slowly, ever so slowly, reversed its downward motion, began to tip back to horizontal. The plasti-nylon ropes were so tight that they vibrated in the arctic wind like some sort of mad Mozart string ensemble. Rock just prayed they wouldn't snap.

The last two dogs of the six-dog team somehow managed to get out of the water with the sled. They shook and shivered off the most water they could, yelping and tangling the lines as they barked for their friends still swimming nose deep in the turgid steaming waters.

Rockson saw a dog stop swimming and go under. In a moment he came to the surface, belly up—dead. Then the lead gave out and went limp.

Rockson realized there was no saving the first two dogs. He inched forward and cut the reins. Oxytl yelped out a last, sharp bark and went under, probably more boiled than drowned. Rockson crawled along the ice on his belly, spreading his weight, holding onto a line. He pulled on the reins of the middle two huskies. They emerged from the water dripping like water rats, their fur plastered against their bodies. He punched each of them hard in the chest and, sputtering up lungfuls of water, both started moving.

"There, boys," he said, trying to calm the terrified dogs. "Let's get the hell out of here, fellas, okay?"

Once they realized they were out alive, the dogs rose to their feet and walked alongside Rockson as he carefully moved back toward the river bank.

They had to stop for nearly an hour. Rock dried his

boots over a fire; the huskies were rubbed dry and reattached to their harnesses. Some of the supplies from his sled were moved to the others since he was short two dogs now. Though the men were reeling from the close call, Rockson insisted they push on. His new right lead dog took over instinctively as the "driver" of the others. Just like men, Rock thought grimly, huskies always need one dog who assumes control—or they begin trying to run off in all directions.

Considering all they had been through, the Doomsday Warrior shouldn't have been so surprised when one man couldn't take any more. Robinson went crazy. Robinson's beard had grown wild and scraggly and it was covered with icicles. He started muttering to himself, pulling his sled dangerously close to Rockson's from time to time and shouting obscenities and numerous complaints such as, "You've lost us," and "We're all going to die!"

His eyes were an odd sort of bloodshot orange. Rockson waved the men to a halt finally and they lit a set of torches and sat down in a close circle. Robinson had to be grabbed and set in place by Detroit and Chen, who sat alongside him. Rockson stared at Robinson in the glow of the orange torches. They were in the middle of an absolutely flat whiteness that dropped off like the ends of the earth in all directions.

"Robinson, I know we are all hurting," he tried to reason. "We will get some rest and safety at the Ice City, I am—"

Robinson wouldn't let him finish. He leapt across at Rockson, catching the commander with a mania-

147

cal stranglehold that Rockson had trouble pulling away from. Detroit leapt into the fray and pulled the madman away. Detroit and Robinson, who had been at odds years before, began slamming away at one another. Rockson jumped to his feet and tried to tear them apart. He was surprised that Detroit wouldn't obey him. He just kept pummeling at Robinson, the madman screaming and trying to beat back at the black Freefighter with his frost-chafed, bloody hands. Neither was doing much damage to the other. At last they fell exhausted in the snow. Rockson had an awful feeling that even though this fight was over, there would soon be many more, as the men were already beyond the normal range of human endurance. Strangely, the fight seemed to have the effect of bringing Robinson back to his senses. Rock managed to make the two of them apologize and they set off again. Everyone knew now that it wasn't just the elements, but their own minds that they were fighting. Rock himself, despite his years of mind training and meditation—necessary for his pursuit of the higher martial arts—was feeling wretched. He tried to shake a growing brooding melancholy, but couldn't.

At last they came to a valley between two hills, the first hills made of Mother Earth—or at least frozen tundra—that they had seen for days. There were even trees: short squat evergreens.

"The Ice City lies just a few miles more," Tinglim said, "Just on the other side of the Sasquatch Forest!"

Chapter 16

Rockson and his men camped in a sheltered valley where they would be protected from the buffeting wind and driving snow, just outside the Sasquatch Forest. While the tents were being pitched, Rockson and Tinglim took inventory of their supplies. Then, at the meeting he called, Rock told the men, "All the tenting and hunting equipment is sound, and we've got plenty of fuel for the portable stoves. But we've used up the last of the food." The tired men hardly looked interested.

"Well, men," Rockson asked. "Do I have any volunteers for a hunting party?" Tinglim volunteered but Rock vetoed it. "We all know how hard you've worked on this trip. I can tell you're exhausted. Rest. There must be men who are up to it more."

Tinglim nodded. He added, "At least game is plentiful in this area. We can drink tea," Tinglim said somewhat despondently, "until our hunters return." McCaughlin had once again set up the

149

portable stove in the main tent, and set a pot of tea on. But stomachs ached for food.

"Any other volunteers?" asked Rockson.

"I'd like to go," said McCaughlin. "If there's no food there's nothing more for me to do around here."

Robinson suggested, "He'll need a man along who knows what he's doing." He stroked his red beard. "I'm all right now, sir, I swear it."

"Are you volunteering, Robinson?" asked Rockson.

"I guess I am."

"Good," said Rockson heartily. "That settles it. You and McCaughlin will be our hunting party. Synchronize your watches. I want you two back in six hours, whether you've bagged any game for the pot or not. The rest of you men can use this time"—the men groaned—"to get some shut-eye!"

McCaughlin and Robinson checked out the dogs in no time and loaded the sleds with hunting gear and rifles. The dogs, feeling the lightness of the load, in spite of their long travels were frisky and energetic. Soon the hunters vanished from view of the camp in the direction of the forest.

The scattered short, squat evergreens became very abundant as McCaughlin and Robinson rode. The height of the trees increased. After a half-hour, Robinson pulled over and dismounted. McCaughlin found him examining tiny footprints in the snow.

"Hare tracks," said Robinson. His blue eyes flashed with excitement. "Over there are fox tracks, hot on their trail," he said, pointing to prints that looked like those of a small dog. "I propose we follow them wherever they take us in the forest. We can arrange a chain of loopline traps on the hare's route of travel. That way we might snare the hare, or its hunter, the fox.''

"Well, I suppose you know what you are doing," answered McCaughlin. "But this terrain already gives me the creeps. There's something sick-looking about this forest. I propose we travel for an hour more and then, no matter what happens, stop. We can check and collect the traps on our way back." Robinson agreed.

Thus, setting the traps and loops at frequent intervals, they traveled deeper still into the brooding forest. Though the place made McCaughlin uneasy, he was glad he had come along. Robinson *did* know what he was doing, and McCaughlin was learning a lot. The old red-beard displayed an icy calm and cool professionalism as he laid the traps. In light of his blow-up with Rockson, it was easy to see that this was good therapy for Robinson. McCaughlin was also thinking that this might be good therapy for himself.

For Robinson, after the total whiteness of the landscape for days, it was a relief to see the dark green trees and other signs of life. Robinson quickly laid eight traps. At the end of an hour they turned back, to hopefully collect their catch.

The first two traps they checked were empty, but the third bore fruit. A fox! It had struggled valiantly to escape, but in the effort to get its leg out had burrowed its head in the snow and had become frozen fast by its own dying breath. The snow was stained with the fox's blood. As Robinson was prying open the trap to extract it, McCaughlin said, "You know, I can't get rid of this feeling of being watched. It sounds silly, but—" McCaughlin's words were interrupted by a whoosh of a rope flung by unseen hands. It fell around his neck and then was pulled taut. His body was already being dragged away when Robinson stood up holding his catch. He was about to reply as another rope came around his neck too, and pulled him backward along the snow . . .

Rockson lay silent. He tried to meditate, to bring himself to the innermost recesses of his mind. But he couldn't. He was distracted by the eerie-sounding Arctic wind and by the deep regular breathing and snoring of the exhausted hungry men all around him.

He opened his eyes; noticed a light playing on the tent, shining through its coarse fibers. The northern lights, that's all. For a second it had startled him.

He struggled to return to an unremembered dream. He tried to channel his thoughts in the direction of Rona and Kim. Pleasant thoughts. But his mind kept coming back to the deteriorating condition of his men. All had sore, strained, tired muscles and backs stiff from having to stay in one position so long on the sleds. Farrell's and Detroit's hands and feet were covered with chilblains and some frostbite. All had faces burned by the constant icy wind. Their noses were peeling and their faces were cracked with the cold. Pedersen had had a trembling fit and suffered from shortness of breath. Tinglim's salves, ointments, and medicines had been invaluable under the grueling circumstances, and had provided relief. But they were all close to cracking, like Robinson had.

Even though Robinson had recovered, it was a sign of things to come, if they got no respite. Tempers flared; one's mind played tricks. All Arctic adventurers had reported this phenomenon. Was it the very cold, the raw numbing cold that wouldn't go away, or was it the icy sterile environment of snow, wind and ice?

Rock checked his chronometer. *Seven hours* had passed since the hunting party had left camp. Rock was worried. What had become of them?

He decided that a walk outside might clear his brain of the muzziness he'd felt. He found Tinglim outside staring at the sky.

"I don't like the look of that," Tinglim said, pointing to the northern lights that danced above them transforming the white world of reality into rainbows of blue-green fantasy.

"I don't like the feel of it," said Rockson.

Tinglim agreed, "It's the sort of northern lights that awaken the Sasquatch. Why, even the dogs are affected."

Rockson turned to the huddled dogs, saw their wide-eyed look and laid-back ears. They were uneasy, all right. "The hunting party was due back an hour ago," Rockson said. "I think we should go after them—now."

Shortly thereafter, a party composed of Tinglim, Archer, Rockson, Pedersen, and Chen headed out over the snow. Detroit and Scheransky were left to watch camp. The aurora borealis raged across the sky like some demented electrical demon seizing the imagination of even the dullest of creatures below and projecting fear from the starry vault of heaven. Electric blues, greens, and purples assumed grotesque shapes—monsters crouching, writhing, creeping, ready to ambush one's very soul. A feeling of dread anxiety filled the men who rode into the night. This hypnotic light was the source of irrationality. Something that challenged their rational minds, threatening insanity. It was with profound relief that they came under cover of the deep forest.

It was not long before Tinglim discovered the hunting party's tracks and the traps. In less than an hour, the heavy drag marks in the snow were discovered also. They followed these for about a half-mile. Soon, in the distance could be seen a glow that seemed to be emanating from the mouth of a cave. Rock and his men dismounted their sleds to investigate on foot. They climbed the small hill of loose scree and, hidden by a copse of trees, watched shadows cross the light in the cave opening. Rockson motioned his men to go inside.

With their flashlights lit, they advanced through the mouth of the cave. "You'll have to be very careful," Rockson admonished. "Avoid the stalactites and stalagmites. Some of them look damn sharp."

It was like an obstacle course. The cave narrowed down and forced them to go single file. Chen spotted a bit of rag from McCaughlin's jacket on one of the sharp green stalactites. The cave narrowed more and the ceiling lowered; they found themselves crouching.

Deep inside the winding cave, Rock was the first to

notice something peculiar. A smell. Foul, musky. The dogs had sort of a musky scent which he had grown used to, but this was a *putrid* odor that now assaulted his olfactory sense. Something he had never smelled before. Something like rancid human perspiration, or a thousand sweat socks moldering in gym lockers that had just been opened after a hundred years of sitting idle.

"That is Sasquatch smell," gasped out Tinglim.

Rock led the way as they climbed down into another narrow passageway. From time to time they doused their lights to follow the flickering glow. This new tunnel was not limestone like the other passageways, but seemed carved out of dark rock. Trickles of muddy runoff water ran through the pebbly brown dirt underfoot. They were deep under the mountain now, perhaps a quarter mile in, and still descending. The steep pebbly ground slowed their progress and didn't do their attempt at being quiet any good. They were almost at their goal: The glow ahead was bright enough to light their way, so they flicked off their flashlights.

A scream that caused neck hairs to quiver and stand erect, issued from somewhere ahead. It was a scream that sent adrenaline through Rock's body making his heart pound in his ears—it was a scream that could waken the dead, the sound of an animal in exquisite agony. Slowly, cautiously, Rockson and his team progressed toward that orange light ahead and the source of the scream. The floor of the cave grew smoother, as if worn by the tread of many feet. The ceiling heightened to nine feet or more, and the horrid smell grew overwhelmingly strong.

Rockson stopped without warning; Chen thudded into him, almost pushing Rockson off a ledge. They were twenty feet above the floor of a high dome-ceilinged circular chamber. As they knelt down to keep out of sight, their eyes beheld a gruesome scene. "Easy, men," Rockson whispered.

Robinson, or rather what was left of him, was being roasted on a spit by immense red-haired creatures that resembled orangutans. Five pointy-headed Sasquatch were waiting to taste the flesh of their roasted victim.

"It must have been Robinson's scream," whispered Chen. Rockson nodded. Against the far wall of the chamber lay McCaughlin, bound and gagged, a look of horror on his face as he waited *his* turn on the barbecue spit.

McCaughlin's parka was torn and bloodied, and his neck had a welt—from some sort of rope burn, Rock surmised. Their big friend had to be rescued—now. But to do that, the rescuers would have to do battle. There was no way to get to McCaughlin except through the whole mess of eaters. And the red-furred, pointy-headed things wouldn't like that at all.

Rock sized up his opponents. He could see them clearly in the light of the cooking fire. They were sitting on their haunches, yet even in this position they were as tall as a man. "They must be nine feet tall if an inch," Rock whispered to Chen, who was on the ground alongside him, taking in the gruesome spectacle.

"Yeah, and each one of those buggers weighs in at four hundred pounds, I'll bet," Chen answered uncomfortably. "But a star knife or two might cut them down to size. If I can just hit the right place."

Rock replied, "You do that, Chen. But don't try it from here. They're so busy eating, we might be able to get closer. Close enough to use our shotpistols *and* your star knives. The closer we get before they spot us, the more likely it is they won't get a chance to slaughter McCaughlin."

With Rockson in the lead, the men moved along the ledge, until they found sufficient roughness to the twenty feet of rockface below to afford them footholds. They descended, quite out in the open. Should any of the Sasquatch have turned from their grim repast, they would have seen them. But the monsters were too busy eating. Rock and his men spread out fast, rushed at the things. When they turned, dropping their burned-human supper, the Freefighters began blasting them. Two fell.

"Rapid fire," yelled Rockson, his voice echoing through the subterranean chamber. "Aim for their chests. Don't let 'em grab ya."

The creatures leapt to the fight, having picked up their crude but massive weapons—pikes and axes of the most primitive sort. Chen yelled out, "Rock, here come two more of 'em!"

"Damn," the Doomsday Warrior muttered. The present bunch of opponents was enough trouble! There in the light of the cooking fire, in the smell of human flesh burning, the creatures of the Arctic night and the human invaders faced off.

Rock was confronted by the biggest of the bunch, who wielded an ax that could have taken a chunk out of a truck. The chipped stone head of the thing, secured to a wooden handle, was the size of a man's arm. It swished by Rock as he dove to the left and fired up and sideways, catching the man-thing in the rib cage with a burst of hellfire.

The exploding pellets dug into the Sasquatch and did their work, disintegrating the thing's torso into spinning bloody chunks that splattered across the chamber. The thing heaved to the ground, half afire. Rock headed toward McCaughlin, to free him.

Chen hit his target not with a blast of his shotpistol, but with something even more deadly— an exploding star knife. The martial-arts expert's whizzing death-dealer caught a Sasquatch in mid-roar, right in its throat. The roar turned to a gurgle as the five-pointed metal star dug into its vocal cords. Then, when the explosive tips of the star knife exploded, the huge red-furred head blew off the body of the monster and slammed against the ceiling of the chamber. The headless body of the cave being staggered forward, its huge hairy arms flailing, blood fountaining from its neck. Then it fell with a *whump.* "Good shot, Chen," the Doomsday Warrior yelled. But the Freefighters still faced five of the man-eaters. And they were augmented by two more nasty fellows who appeared on the ledge above. Each of the new buddy-boys carried boulders poised over their heads, held by their huge hairy arms. They had every intention of crushing the invaders, and then eating them too.

Wham! A boulder was tossed, slamming down into the hard dirt just to the left of Rockson. Another boulder momentarily flew above and then crashed right next to Archer. The throwers melted into the shadows.

Where were they? Rock wondered as he tried to sight up the elusive creatures in the half-light. "Random fire, full automatic," he yelled, but the Freefighters were already sending out a hail by the time he finished speaking. Rock decided to play hero and shot out from his concealment. He zigzagged thirty yards up the underground chamber, narrowly missing getting caught by a monstrous boulder thrown from above. He dove behind a trapezoid-shaped stalagmite. Rockson rolled out, his shotpistol in hand, and came to a standing position.

He had found the source of the boulders. There! Twenty feet above him was a grinning Sasquatch. It was beating on its broad chest. It snarled and let out a stream of steam from its nostrils into the cold cavern air. And then it grabbed up a desk-sized boulder and began to throw it. Tinglim threw his harpoon at the creature. It stuck in the broad chest and the thing's eyes rolled up, its pitch of death altered enough to just miss the Doomsday Warrior.

The concussion of the shattering boulder shook the cavern as Rock was showered with sharp rock fragments. Then another opponent jumped down. Rockson stood his ground and stared into the red, veiny eyes, as big as coffee mugs.

The creature stared back. It was the biggest, ten feet tall. This Sasquatch had a thick pelt of orange hair, not red. Its wide skull and flat face ended up in a point, sort of like a dunce cap at the crown of his head. But there was no mistaking it: despite the primitive hunger and hostility in those red eyes, there was another element—intelligence. The thing was doubly dangerous therefore.

"Greeefffffffffhhhh!" the Sasquatch growled, its

159

wet nostrils flaring, its eyes growing wild and impatient. There was a thin trickle of saliva running down that massive red, hairy jaw. Teeth appeared but the sides of the mouth weren't parted. It was more like hunger than friendship. The thing edged forward and Rock began quick dancing steps backward.

Suddenly the thing leapt, and Rock did a flip backward, landing on his feet. It would have made Chen proud.

That seemed to be about enough for the hulking half-human, and it rushed forward trying to engulf the Freefighter in a bear hug to the death. But Rock was too fast, stepping sideways in a Pa-kua movement.

The Sasquatch was left clutching air. And he got even madder when Rockson delivered a kick to its knee—or what he hoped was its knee. It howled *"Frekkkkkk!"* Rock thought it might mean "Now I kill and eat you, but first I pluck your arms and legs."

It stood and stared at Rockson, becoming absolutely motionless, frozen like a holgraphic snapshot, its every sense of perception focused on the Freefighter. Its red, wide-slitted eyes were a furnace, filled with incendiary flames of anger. The Doomsday Warrior could practically feel the heat emanating from them. A black tongue, thick as a man's wrist, darted in and out of the open jaw, as if it was tasting Rockson's scent. And evidently it liked what it tasted. It rested back down on its haunches preparing what Rockson could see was a new leap.

Without turning, Rock sensed the presence of another—a human—to his right side.

"Move real slow, Chen," Rock whispered. "This thing's looking dinner right in the eye. I don't think it's going to watch you too hard. Circle to the left."

"I'll take a shot at it. I think my star knife can do the trick," the Freefighter said. Chen moved almost imperceptibly to the side, out of the direct striking range of the thing.

"Not yet," Rock said as he moved ever so slowly to the opposite side. He moved with trained fighting instincts, honed down over the years. Rockson was a pure fighting machine, a survivor. The Doomsday Warrior had withstood all that the cruel Post-Nuke world could hurl at him. But he knew in his heart that someday something would come at him that would be too powerful—and he would die. This might be that day.

But Rock didn't feel like taking an endless snooze in the Arctic today. This monster was going to have to die, not him. He kept his eyes directly on the creature's own burning saucers, looking for the sudden flicker that meant attack. But the Sasquatch was in no hurry. Its hunting instincts had taken over, and it stood frozen, its big mitt-sized hands raised up, its apelike snout pointing like a hunting dog straight at the Doomsday Warrior. The red eyes followed Rockson as he moved, letting Chen lift the star knife and prepare to hurl it . . . The Sasquatch grew impatient, sprang into the air uncoiling those enormous legs, and headed straight toward Rockson's throat. The hairy hands tried to close around the Doomsday Warrior's neck in one swift grab. Chen couldn't throw for fear of hitting Rock.

Rock sensed the Sasquatch's attack just a split

second before it came. He dove sideways, flying through the icy cavern, landing flat on his stomach ten feet away. The thing's hairy hands squeezed shut on the spot where the Doomsday Warrior had been standing.

It snarled in frustration, its eyes setting again on its target. The immense mouth opened, emitting a howl of fury. The Sasquatch came bearing down on Rock again.

"Now, Chen!" Rock yelled, jumping aside as Chen threw his weapon. The star knife flew accurately into the thing's bowels, which exploded in a rain of red guts.

Three other Sasquatch ran in, letting out with a chorus of bellowing roars that echoed and reverberated in the Freefighters' ears. But from behind the new looming red-haired figures came a black form with a fire—something Sasquatch-sized and mean—*Archer!* A flaming arrow shot from his crossbow caught the closest Sasquatch squarely in the belly. It sank in deep, and set the thing's thick hair on fire. The Sasquatch tried to pull the hook-tipped arrow out but every time it yanked, the serrated hook-tip made it scream in pain. The thing ran around ablaze, slamming against the rock walls, its burning, smoking flesh brightening the scene.

"Meeee goood!" said Archer, removing yet a second self-igniting steel arrow from the quiver on his back and notching it onto his taut crossbow string. But before Archer could finish, another still-active monster was upon him, swinging a huge ax—sharp edge forward—at the human giant. Archer deflected the first two blows, but the third swing

162

smashed into his hair-matted skull and splashed red all over his face. The ax stuck there, and Archer slid to the floor gurgling up a red paste. His eyes rolled upward.

Rock took to the air, using a two-legged kick against the icy rock wall to hurl his body forward, somersaulting into the Sasquatch's huge form. It was as if seeing Archer fall had driven Rock to new heights of anger-energy. The Sasquatch actually was staggered by Rock's blow. Chen, for his part, capitalized on its stunned condition by raising his Liberator and letting out a stream of slugs—the last of his clip. The bullets bit into the half-human, cutting a bloody seam up the center of his chest like a pair of scissors. It fell and rolled away along the cavern's floor and out of sight.

Rockson raised his hunting knife—not much of a weapon—as one of the remaining attackers shot forward like a meteor and slammed Rock to the ground. The big knife spiraled through the air like a wounded bird and fell in the frozen dirt yards away. Pedersen poured out the hot lead from his shotpistol, though, and took the creature down.

The last three Sasquatch stepped forward in the semidarkness, flickers of the declining cooking fire lighting their ugly faces. One seemed to snicker, like a human does when he's just pulled a royal flush in a poker game. Rock was picking himself up slowly; dazed, vulnerable. It evidently thought Rock was about to cash in his chips—and so did the Doomsday Warrior. It came forward, a crude ax raised in its hair-covered hand. Rock groggily rolled to the side to avoid the blow but the thing was good at axing—it

163

whipped the ax in an arc, striking backhand at Rock. The side of the stone blade caught the Doomsday Warrior just on the side of the skull and he fell backward, staggering, almost falling unconscious. His eyes were spinning around in his head like balls on a roulette wheel, and he could feel a stream of blood flowing down his neck. He blinked, trying to regain his vision. He couldn't go under—not with that hairy man-beast coming at him. Suddenly it was McCaughlin to the rescue. He had been cut free by Chen. "I got him, Rock," the Scotsman yelled. He struck out with a roundhouse kick that could demolish a cinder-block wall—and had, in several practice sessions back at Century City. The blow was aimed at the wrist of the ax-holding hand. The ax spun loose and Rock caught it. Before the Sasquatch could take a step, Rock swung down with both arms and buried the sharp end into the forehead of the Sasquatch with every ounce of strength he possessed. Its eyes flew out in a gush of yellow fluid as it fell to its knees. Pieces of bone and flesh scattered all over the killing field. Its head was split in two. The last two Sasquatch alive hightailed it.

Rock's lungs hurt more than his body. The pain of sucking in the icy air as he fought, the pain of his many injuries, were now the dictator of his numb world. The Doomsday Warrior tried to stay on his feet and started walking toward the blood-soaked figure of Archer. His vision clouded. He felt the throbbing pain in his skull from the ax blow turn into a hammering whirlpool of blackness—and he fell into it.

Chapter 17

Rock awoke several hours later, and realized he was moving. The pale Arctic sun on the horizon let him see that he was on the sled again, this time lying under a mound of blankets and pelts. The driver of the sled was McCaughlin. "Where?" Rock asked.

"We're through the woods and on our way to Ice City," McCaughlin answered cheerfully. "As far as we can tell, you're in one piece," he went on. "You might want to move around a bit to see if any bones are broken. You took quite a blow—but you'll live. Thanks for the rescue, buddy!"

Rock carefully moved an inch under the blanket. He felt soreness but no stinging pains. Arms, legs, fingers, toes—all were in good working order.

"Archer . . . is he? . . ."

"No, he's alive—but barely," McCaughlin said with concern. "We bandaged up his skull, pushing the bone together, and sealed it with plasti-salve. But I don't know—the ax entered his brain."

"Maybe," Rock said, "he can be helped at Ice City."

"Don't talk . . . Here, sip some of this Foxmeat broth—the Sasquatch just threw it aside: they preferred human meat. Robinson caught the fox just before we were captured. You've been unconscious for hours. I skinned it and cooked up a stew. We've all had some."

"Thanks," Rock murmured as he pushed the cup to his lips. He didn't care what the hell it had in it. He needed some energy. He sipped the cup of tepid brew down and half swallowed, half chewed the bits of meat in it. When he'd finished he asked, "What was the total damage?"

"Everyone except Archer is okay. Of course, Robinson was—"

"I know," said Rock. "What else?"

"The damned Sasquatch that survived ran out of the cave and found our sleds. They took three sleds complete with dog teams when they hightailed it."

"How far to the Ice City?"

"I'm not sure," admitted McCaughlin.

Rock tried to sit up, and managed. His face was cold. He wrapped the flaps of the huge furry hood closer around his face, only letting his nose and eyes show. "Where's the map?"

"Under the blanket. Near where your right hand was." Rock groped around until he found the bundle, drew it out from under the blanket and unrolled it in his lap. He quickly found the edge of the Sasquatch Forest and, doing a little figuring based on McCaughlin's compass reading and the number of hours they had traveled, decided they were only ten miles or so from Ice City.

*　　*　　*

They sped through the snow-covered forest of dark majestic evergreens with trunks as huge as the redwoods of California. It wasn't long till the party began traveling steadily upward. They must have gradually ascended a few thousand feet, when the forest stopped abruptly and they were on a plateau of snow and ice—entering a mist. They moved ahead, slowly, hardly able to see. Suddenly the mist cleared, and the small band stared down at the most fantastic sight any of them had ever seen.

"Behold!" said Tinglim, exultantly. "There is the Ice City!"

Chapter 18

"I can't believe it," said McCaughlin, pulling his sled up alongside Tinglim's. Below them, built on a frozen lake that filled the mile-wide crater of a long-dead volcano, was a frost-covered city of spires and towers. All the buildings were made of ice—over a hundred buildings, of every size, all shining like frosted glass.

There was traffic along the winding streets: great sleighs filled with people and pulled by horse-sized elks; sleds of every size and description filled with furs, foods, clothes; all moving around the fabulous metropolis.

At the far end of the crater, half up the lip, a spired castle rose like a diamond dream. "The Potala," said Tinglim. "That's what they call the palace. The king of the Ice People, Yiglim, lives a life of luxury there!"

As they snapped the whips and their teams rode down into the valley, Rock heard the strains of a distant organ—unearthly, awe-inspiring.

They reached level ground and rode through the

city's main gate. The inhabitants were noticing them now. The Eskimo types turned from their rounds in the street and waved.

It was a beautiful little city. Rock realized now that it was not simply white. There were the palest of pastel colors to many of the buildings, glowing in the cracks of sun spilling through the clouds above. Brightly colored pennants waved from pale azure minarets, pastel-pink spiraled towers, and faintly golden turrets.

The strains of the deep-throated organ grew louder as they passed a Gothic-style cathedral with steeples of many-colored splendor. The music came from there. It rolled and echoed through the icy streets.

The sleds went right under arching jets of water shot from twin sculptures—sea lions carved out of solid ice! The huskies were barking excitedly at the commotion of people and the yelping of other dogs around the city. They strained against the harness as they pulled the gliding sleds down the main approach to the castle, between two white walls of snow.

In the courtyard of the Potala, they were greeted by ten white-garmented "snow guards" armed with spears. Though the guards didn't seem to expect a fight, they still visibly relaxed when Tinglim spoke and explained in his native tongue who they were.

Tinglim turned to Rockson, "It is all right. They are friendly to my tribe. Now that they know who we are, we will be welcomed, fed, and treated as guests." He smiled. "It is as I said, Rockson. I did not steer you wrong."

"Good, Tinglim. You did well," Rock replied,

realizing that Tinglim was digging for some praise here. "But tell them we have a seriously wounded man with us. Tell them I implore them to do anything they can do for Archer."

Tinglim led one of the Ice City guards to Archer's sled. The man peered down at Archer. He was visibly shaken when Tinglim lifted the bandage on the giant Freefighter's head. The man said something to Tinglim which Tinglim translated. "He says we must rush this man to the Crystal infirmary. There he will stand a chance of survival. I can go with Archer—while you go to the king's palace and wait there for news," Tinglim volunteered.

"No, I want to see this infirmary. My pal has to have the best of care. I'll come with you and Archer. The rest of you men—Scheransky, you too—follow these friends. Get some chow, or whatever else they have to offer." Rockson felt much less woozy now, and got off the sled.

Tinglim and Rockson watched as the guards placed Archer gently on a stretcher, and then walked alongside as the men carried Archer to one of the side buildings in the palace courtyard, a single-story building of translucent pink ice that looked like a quartz crystal.

Once inside, they found themselves under a vaulted ceiling faced with a maze of corridors—all of translucent ice—that seemed to glow of their own accord. They were led by an orderly to the operating theater, a pentagonal chamber of thirty odd feet in diameter, the center of which contained a table. The table was, as far as Rockson could see, the only thing not made of ice. The guards were instructed to lay the wounded man upon the table by two shaven-headed Eskimo men wearing pale blue uniforms. Each of these men wore an elaborate crystal necklace. Their authoritative and professional manner seemed to indicate that they were doctors of some sort.

The doctors bent over Archer and placed the ends of the crystal necklaces against the wounded man's face and body at various points. The crystal necklaces seemed to come to life, sparkling and glowing with multi-colored reflection.

One of the doctors spoke to Tinglim.

"This man is very ill," Tinglim translated. "The doctors do not know if they can save him. But it might be possible with the use of crystal accumulator."

"Tell them to try," Rock said gravely. He didn't have the slightest idea what a crystal accumulator was, but Archer was turning blue and his breathing was shallow. The wound would have long ago proved fatal to a lesser man.

Tinglim told the doctor what Rockson had said. The doctors went into action, moving their hands over a control panel of some sort in a corner of the room. There was a ringing in Rockson's ear, then a low hum. The floor vibrated. Rock watched in amazement as a huge part of the ceiling, filled with countless multifaceted crystals, began lowering toward the table.

The towering mass of crystals had a recess in them the size of a table. The whole apparatus slowly engulfed Archer. Then the crystals started to give off pleasant tinging sounds and began glowing in many colors, each crystal winking on and off like a

Christmas tree bulb.

"That is the crystal accumulator," said Tinglim. "It will begin tapping the earth's magnetic sphere and channeling that energy into Archer. It will— hopefully—speed the reknitting of his tissues. The doctors say it will take days."

"Won't Archer starve? Won't he need water?" asked Rockson, a bit in awe at this surprising sign of advanced technology.

Tinglim replied, "No. The crystal accumulator will provide all sustenance. We must leave now. The doctors will turn up the power to maximum, and it is dangerous to be around when it is at full power."

Not knowing what else to do, the Doomsday Warrior left the fallen Freefighter in the charge of the good doctors, and with Tinglim joined the rest of his men at the Ice Palace gate.

The beautiful Crystal infirmary was to the Potala what a dimestore gem is to a thirty-five carat diamond. The palace, though twenty stories high, had the appearance of lightness and the delicacy of a confection. It actually glowed. Its hundreds of delicately constructed Gothic spires were a pale pastel rainbow of color. The windows were filled with ice "stained glass" and the walls were so translucent that one could see figures moving about inside the hundreds of rooms.

"Shall we go in?" asked Tinglim. "The king knows we are here, and it is best not to let him wait too long."

Rock motioned the others to follow them up the sixteen ice steps and through the open doorway. White robed men led them through the main hallway. The cathedral-like ceiling above was filled with gargoyles and demons carved from frozen ice. The floor beneath them was inlaid with marbled ice tiles. Delicate snowflake tapestries adorned the walls. Only the chairs and tables were not made of ice. Nearly everything in this Ice City world had been chipped into existence.

Rockson noticed it immediately when he came into the vast—and cold—audience room of the Ice King: *The gloom.* There were no smiles on the faces of the dozen or so court officials who lined up near the entrance to greet the strangers. The officials politely bowed and Rockson nodded his greetings to each of them, taking in the elaborate rainbow-dyed furs they wore with some amazement.

The head official, wearing a particularly long expression, parlayed with Tinglim, who translated: "The king is unhappy because his son is missing. He went out alone—far out to the east of the city to hunt the white fox. It is a Vision Quest all young men must do as they come of age. He is days late in returning. So far, search parties have failed to locate him. He is just sixteen years of age. An only son, the heir to the throne . . . And he is feared to be dead."

"I see," said Rockson. "That explains all this glumness."

A hush came over the great hall as the Ice King entered and strode down the royal ermine carpet to his carved ice throne. He was Eskimo featured, but tall and lean, perhaps forty years of age. He was dressed in red velvet and wore a crown of quartz crystals—or diamonds, Rock couldn't tell which. The gems caught and refracted the light like prisms

174

scattering tiny spectra of light as he walked. In his footsteps walked a page, perhaps nine or ten years of age, carrying a white fox fur. As they approached the steps to the throne, the boy scurried ahead of the king, ran up the steps, and after placing the fur on the throne took his place behind it. The king turned and sat on his throne. His grim expression belied the sparkle of his jewels.

Bidden by the king, Rock and Tinglim walked up to the throne. "It is customary to kneel," Tinglim whispered just before he knelt down on one knee. Rockson bowed his head in acknowledgment of the king, but did not kneel. He had never knelt for anyone and he wasn't going to start now. The king didn't seem to mind, for he nodded his head abruptly and motioned them to come closer. Tinglim and Rock did as the king had ordered.

Rock started to say how glad he was to meet the king and how honored he was, but the king dismissed this with a wave of his hand. He was clearly in no mood for formalities. Rockson tried the direct approach. "We need supplies—more sleds, food, and an experienced guide or two that know the land to the north of here. We are on the trail of a killer, a beast who is intent on destroying the world. His name is Killov. He has killed many of Tinglim's people and uncounted thousands of my people. And now he has a weapon that has the capability of annihilating any chance for freedom in the world. Will you help us?"

Tinglim translated. The grim set of the king's jaw did not change. He stared stonily into the distance as he answered. Tinglim translated. "Rockson, the Ice

King refuses to help you. Nothing will be done, no work of any kind. No entertainment, no show of cheer, is to be allowed in this city until his son's safe return."

Rockson was aghast. *If the son dies?* he thought. "Tinglim, you *must* impress upon the king the urgency of our task!"

Tinglim said another string of words to the king, punctuating his words by urgent gestures in the air. The king appeared unmoved and said the one word that Rockson didn't have to have translated. "No."

The king dismissed them with a wave of his hand. Two heavyset guards in royal purple robes escorted the petitioners away. The audience with the king was over.

The whole weary hungry party were led to a side hall which had been prepared in advance for dinner. Twenty nobles and their ladies were already seated at the hundred-foot-long table awaiting the team members' arrival. The ladies all looked like Muglig, Rockson's bed-friend, and wore white fur robes over their slim brown bodies. They wore their shiny jet-black hair in elaborate bejeweled braids. And their nails were long and painted white. The noblemen wore red-dyed sealskin frocks with gathered silk—or what appeared to be silk—collars. Impressed by their finery, Rockson realized for the first time how scruffy his band must look. None of them had had a chance to bathe since they started out on the trek. They looked and smelled like hell.

The team members joined the assemblage at the long table and with a minimum of pleasantry launched into the dinner. They shoveled away at the candied lichen and vegetable roots. They tunneled through succulent mounds of roast yak. They consumed oceans of wine served by older women attendants, who didn't speak, and broke off huge hunks of doughy bread to mop up the gravy. The lords and ladies were delighted by their enthusiasm and ate heartily themselves. Only Rockson maintained a semblance of decorum, eating his food with less than his usual gusto.

"You must eat more food to keep up your strength," prodded Tinglim. "The lords and ladies are concerned that you don't like their food." But Rockson was lost in thought. How was he to go on without supplies? Suddenly a male attendant rushed in. Word had come that the ruler's son had been found. They all adjourned at once to the throne room.

In the audience room, the messenger fell to his knees, nearly chipping the ice with his impact. The sorrowful messenger breathlessly described firsthand the scene the search party had found.

"Far to the east, we found your son, hanging upside down inside a cave. His body had been badly burned. He had been . . ." The messenger paused to get a hold of himself before he went on, "—mutilated. We cut him down and brought his body home to be buried. We found *these* near the body, Sire." Rock edged to the front of the crowd to get a closer look. The messenger held crushed cigarette butts in his left hand. In his right was a broken handle from one of the instruments of torture. It had writing on it. Rock recognized the Cyrillic writing—it was unmistakably Russian.

Killov! he thought. So now Killov has graduated to butchering children. But what for? Killov had no interest in sex of any kind, perverted or not. Ah—but Killov loved to *watch* his victims as he inflicted pain; or as someone did it for him.

Rockson quickly informed Tinglim of his suspisions, who in turn informed the king. The Eskimo ruler turned to Rockson, his eyes ablaze. "This Killov is the man you spoke of earlier?" Rockson nodded. "This is the man you suspect of mutilating my son?" Rock answered affirmatively. The king's body grew rigid with anger. *"I ... want ... revenge!"* he boomed as he slammed his fist down on the throne's arm like a jackhammer. The king, regaining his control, stared hard at Rockson, as if seeing him for the first time. "I pledge my support for your expedition—under one condition ..." He paused, waiting for Tinglim to translate.

"What is that?" asked Rockson.

"That you do your utmost to do away with this *Killov,*" he said, uttering Killov's name with obvious distaste. "Rid me of this monster that stalks my land."

"I pledge to do so," Rockson said firmly.

"In addition ... I want you to bring me evidence of his death," the king went on.

"What kind of evidence?" Rock asked.

"I want you to bring me this child-defiler's head!"

Rockson was astounded. The thought of carrying Killov's head back to the Ice King was absurd. "We don't do things like that," he protested. "No matter how justified it may seem, if we commit mutilation, then we are no better than Killov."

The king stood bolt upright and towered over Rockson. *"I . . . want . . . his . . . head!"*

Rock stood there for a moment and then turned and looked at Pedersen, the anthropologist, who nodded slightly. "Very well," said Rockson, appearing to give in, though he knew in his heart he could never fulfill his promise.

The king relaxed. "Good! I will resupply you well, and send my most knowledgeable scouts with you. . . ."

The funeral procession—the likes of which none of the Rock team had ever envisioned in their wildest dreams, occurred the next morning. The boy-child of the king in a nearly transparent ice coffin was borne on the shoulders of the palace guard and carried down the main street. Drum rolls filled the air. Candles were lit in the halls of every building and shone through the walls in the eternal northern twilight in a most eerie manner.

The king's sleigh followed directly behind the Ice Prince's bier, pulled by immense wapiti—large elk— their frosty breath filling the air. Behind the sleigh came the ladies and gentlemen of mourning, dressed entirely in black. Rockson and his men, their heads bowed like the others, moved in procession behind the funeral cortege four abreast down the main street.

Just as the solemn candlelit procession reached the ice crypt in a nearby slope, a man stepped out from behind some boulders of colored ice. At first Rockson thought it was makeup, but as the procession closed on the crypt, Rockson realized the man had some sort of icelike skin of the palest blue. His eyes seemed sculpted out of ice—like the sea-lion fountains.

"Who's that?" Rockson whispered to Tinglim.

"The most holy Ice Shaman. He officiates at all funerals."

The pallbearers laid the coffin at the shaman's feet. The king stepped down from his sleigh and stood next to the shaman. The rest of the assemblage grouped around the coffin. Rockson watched as the man of ice threw some black and red particles on the coffin and chanted a dirge filled with infinite sadness. Then he turned and went back behind the ice boulders. The king could hardly contain his grief as the coffin carriers lowered the coffin into the crypt and slid the ice cover over it. Then the funeral horns stopped blowing. The candles and torches of the parade were extinguished save one, which was to be carried back to the palace. One candle in every building was to be kept burning for the official five days of mourning.

The funeral procession broke up and started back to the Ice City. Rockson noticed dozens, hundreds, of ice crypts scattered about the slope. He couldn't help thinking what would happen if a spring thaw ever came to these parts. But that wasn't his problem— time was.

In the near darkness, as he walked with the king back toward his palace, Rockson, whose keen senses should have detected any pursuer, felt an unexpected icy hand on his shoulder. He steeled himself for battle and turned. But it was the Ice Priest. The man's blue face was close enough to feel his frosty breath.

The fingers like icicles withdrew. The Ice Shaman's garments, though made of ice, seemed to bend and flow like a regular robe. In a low grating voice he said, "I must speak to you, stranger."

"I don't have the time," Rockson said.

After Tinglim had translated, the king urgently whispered something to Tinglim. Tinglim translated, "You *must* speak to the holy shaman. The king begs you not to refuse him his right to interrogate strangers." Rockson realized he might be jeopardizing the entire mission if he refused. The king himself seemed to be in awe of the Ice Shaman.

"Very well," the Freefighter said with a sigh, letting himself be led back behind the monstrous blue ice boulder from whence the man had come. Behind the boulder was a narrow entrance, and Rockson had to stoop to follow the short Ice Shaman into a large dimly lit room carved from ice. It was much like the king's own throne room. There the Ice Shaman took a seat and bid Rockson sit facing him in the Ice City equivalent of a Morris wing chair. Tinglim sat on a stool between them and translated.

"What do you want of me?" asked Rockson. "I have much to do . . ." By the light of twelve candles, Rock explained his mission.

When he had finished, the Ice Shaman remained silent for a long time, and then said, *"So what* if Killov destroys the world? This would not be the first time such a thing has happened, Rockson. Many civilizations have existed on this earth. The last one to destroy itself with atomic weapons was Atlantis, over nine thousand years ago. They managed to sink their entire continent with the force of their nuclear bombs."

"You say there really was an Atlantis?" Rockson asked. "We only know of the ancient Egyptian civilization. Everything that existed before that appears to have vanished, leaving no trace."

"Not so, Rockson. You see, the survivors of the Atlantean civilization found their way into the hollow part of the earth—you can sometimes reach it through a tunnel that periodically opens at the exact location of the north pole. There, gravity bends and one can actually walk sideways quite a distance into the earth. The survivors of Atlantis, in order to flee radioactivity, which was much greater by far than that caused by World War Three, entered the underworld. There they stayed, living like cave bats for thousands of years, carefully maintaining much of their old knowledge. They emerged from the underworld to reclaim their planet, only to find that the devolved mutations of their war ruled the land they had once claimed as their own. These devolved beings are the Sasquatch.

"The Atlanteans, physically, were no match for them, having grown weak from their safety underground. The Atlanteans had destroyed all their old weapons in their long stay under the earth. They had become peaceful but weak. But the surface was a fierce place. In the struggle to survive, the Atlanteans lost much of their knowledge.

Do you know that we, the human race—the Eskimo and the Indians of the north, the Russians and Americans—are *all* the great-great-grandchildren of those Atlanteans? And we have the same flaw—we are inventive. So inventive that we had another war, for we were inventive without being mentally at peace." The shaman smiled. His teeth tinkled.

"Even if what you say is true, it's all the *more* reason for stopping Killov. We've got to stop the use of any more weapons of mass destruction."

The shaman smiled, and Rockson saw what appeared to be bluish icicles instead of teeth inside his blue-lipped mouth. It was very disturbing to look at. The shaman said, "As long as mankind is not mentally at peace, there will always arise another Killov or Drushkin or Hitler. My advice, Rockson, is to understand that there is a time and place for everything, and that everything happens at the right time. There are many examples in history," he continued, pointing to the great row of books along the walls—real books, but placed on ice shelves.

"But that's just it," replied Rockson. "There is *no* time. As we speak, Killov is approaching his destination. Every precious second wasted brings us all closer to mass destruction." Rock could see he was wasting his breath on the shaman. "I must leave," he said, getting up from his chair.

"Before you leave, you must answer me this riddle," the shaman said.

Rock was chafing at the bit now. He had to get out of there. "What riddle?" he asked impatiently.

The shaman spoke his riddle: "A man who collects compasses lives in a square-shaped green house. He has one and a half wives with four arms and two red faces. His two children are alive, but her child, though living, is not living. The house has five red chimneys and all four sides of the house face south. On a Tuesday in June, the man stares out of one of the house's twenty-three windows and sees a bear walk by. What color is the bear?" The shaman got up from his chair and went to the bookshelf, turning his back on Rockson.

"I honestly don't know or care," said Rockson. "I've had it up to *here!*" Rockson whispered to Tinglim as he put the back of his hand under his chin. By the time the shaman had turned back from the shelf, the Doomsday Warrior was nowhere to be seen.

"He is a rash young man," muttered the shaman.

"He doesn't know our customs," Tinglim replied.

"Nevertheless, he should be taught a lesson." He smiled as he looked upon Tinglim's worried face. "Know ye this. I'll see him again before he leaves. Go. Catch up to him. He needs you."

Rock checked in on Archer's progress at the Crystal infirmary. The doctors said that though Archer's healing powers were remarkable, it would be many days yet before it would be safe to remove him from the crystal accumulator, and weeks before he was fully recovered. Rock hated to leave him behind, but it was in Archer's best interest. It was time to move on.

The extra supplies and sleds Rockson had requested were provided by the Ice King as arranged. Rockson, in the dim light of the winter sun, met the three new men that Tinglim had chosen to go along with them. The Nara chief said, "These men—

Zebok, Ngaicook, and Dalmok—are expert hunters. When we run short of food, their harpoons will provide."

Rockson nodded to the three men, who like Tinglim wore sealskin parkas. They were darker and shorter than Tinglim, barely five feet tall. The first one, Zebok, was the shortest and darkest of the three. His movements were quick and agile. Rock watched him move with interest. He hitched up his sled with great efficiency and speed.

The one called Ngaicook had very slanted eyes, like Chen's and a scar ran the length of his face from the right of his forehead across his flat wide nose and down to the left of his chin. He stared impassively at Rockson, unmoving. *The quiet type*. Well, that's okay, the Doomsday Warrior thought, as long as he's a good hunter and sledsman.

The third one, Dalmok, was all smiles. His two top middle teeth were broken and yellow. This man appeared much older than the first, by about twenty years. His face was a mass of wrinkles like a sunbaked prune. His black eyes seemed merry and flitted about the group of Freefighters. When the man went to his sled and petted the lead dog, a big spitted gray-and-white husky, all the dogs wagged their tails and barked happily.

"Can they shoot too?" Rock asked. "Will they fire upon the enemies of their king, will they shoot at Killov's troops?" Tinglim nodded.

Rockson made sure the antimatter detector was secure on its sled, and he was about to move the reinforced column out when over a dozen shaven-headed acolytes toting spears came running up

185

behind them, yelling and threatening.

Rockson put his hand on his shotpistol handle, but hesitated in drawing it out when he saw the Ice Shaman come up behind the spear holders. The throng parted to let the ice man through. "Why all the spears?" Rock asked.

The Ice Shaman said, "You have insulted me by leaving my presence without my permission. I cannot let you leave Ice City until you make amends."

Rock eyed his Freefighters. They had spread out, and were ready to blast the spearmen and their ice guru to a bloody pulp. But Rockson didn't want violence. "What kind of amends?" he asked, thin-lipped.

"Either," smiled the Ice Shaman, "apologize by getting down on your knees and kissing my feet, or answer the impossible riddle."

Rockson ruled out the former course of action. He hadn't gotten down for Killov, or Vassily, who controlled two thirds of the world. He hadn't knelt before the Ice King. He was not about to kneel to some two-bit icicle. "I'll answer the riddle," said Rockson decisively. "If you don't mind repeating it."

"Good!" answered the shaman, rubbing his hands with glee. "I'll give you all the time you need." He paused for effect and then repeated his riddle. "A man who collects compasses lives in a square-shaped green house. He has one and a half wives with four arms and two red faces. His two children are alive, but her child, though living is not living. The house has five red chimneys and all four sides of the house face south. On a Tuesday in June, the man stares out

186

of one of the house's twenty-three windows and sees a bear walk by. What color is the bear?''

Rockson looked at the spear-toting acolytes. They were a mean-looking bunch who looked more like pirates than holy men. Shrunken heads hung from the center of their amber-bead necklaces. Still, they had only spears, and Rock's men had their shotpistols strapped on as usual. Rockson gave the riddle some time, turning it around in his head.

"Give up?" laughed the shaman. "If so, get on your knees and apologize or you all die." His men raised their spears.

Chen, who had moved close to Rockson, whispered, "We're ready. Don't bow down."

Rock was about to give the order to fire, his hand tightened on his pistol's handle, when the answer flashed across his mind. "The color of the bear is *white!*"

"Excellent!" said the shaman. "You are quite right! Now, it is time for me—and *you*—to go. May the gods be with you on your journey, Rockson." With a wave of the Ice Shaman's hand, the acolytes lowered their spears and gave way on the road. The Ice Shaman walked hurriedly away followed by his men. In a matter of moments they had all disappeared from view.

Later, when they were all on the trail heading north, Chen pulled his sled alongside Rock's and shouted, "How the hell did you know the bear was white? That's the most incredible thing I've ever heard."

"Easy," said Rock. "Any house having all four sides facing south must be at the north pole. And if

187

the house is at the north pole, only a polar bear would be passing it."

"And polar bears are white," said Chen in amazement. "But what about the rest of the riddle? The one and a half wives? The child that is dead but isn't—all that stuff?"

Rockson smiled. "I'm not sure all that wasn't there to obscure the single relevant fact in the riddle."

"But why did he ask the riddle, Rock?" asked Chen more puzzled than ever. "Why did he threaten us? Is the shaman mad?"

"No, he was stalling for time," Rock explained. I think he intended us to wait; he wouldn't let us leave until the proper moment. If you think about it, the whole confrontation lasted only about five minutes. He wasn't interested in fighting at all. He said something to me in the interview I had with him that sticks in my mind. His advice to me was to realize 'there is a time and place for everything and that everything happens at the right time.' He adjusted our place in space-time. He delayed us a few minutes for some reason."

Chapter 19

Chrome was sniffing the air with his enhanced olfactory circuits, circuits that analyzed every molecule. He could detect a herd of caribou to the south. He would pick one off, carry it, and eat it raw, a little each day. It would be all he needed to fuel his trek. He would range far and wide, off the road. Any pursuers of Killov would take advantage of the shortcut the uncharted area held. The clever pursuers would try to cut across the loop that the Alaska highway made. *He* would, Chrome thought. *Rockson* would. It would be the smart thing to do.

The metal man was human in only one way; he had but one emotion left in him that seethed through his brain: Revenge. Back from the grave he had come, back stronger than ever before. Back to kill the man who had blown him apart. Rockson. Rockson was as relentless as Chrome. If anyone was out there, trailing them, it was Rockson.

He let revenge seethe through his body now, encouraging the circuits linked to what remained of his blood and muscle systems to move more swiftly.

Like the wind itself, he ran across the hard, frozen tundra toward the caribou herd. He unslung his Dragunov rifle, and without slacking in speed ran the mile and a half to a ridge overlooking the herd of antlered creatures. He made the journey in three minutes and arrived not out of breath. He sighted the smaller of the herd just as they looked up in astonishment at his metal glinting in a patch of sunlight. They had smelled nothing. Nothing animal; nothing human. Yet something was there. Too late they started to run. The small calf to the side fell, its brain split by a Dragunov long-range bullet. Its blank eyes stared up at Chrome as he hefted it on his shoulder. Blood coating his arms and chest, he walked toward his goal, the mountain. Mount Draco.

Chrome, when he was but a human soldier for the empire, had been a skilled mountain climber. But that training in the German Alps hadn't prepared him for the treacherous climb up the peak the map designated as Draco. Draco, at 10,000 meters in height, dwarfed the Alpine peaks he had been trained on. And always there had been a rope connecting him to other climbers for safety. But now the man who had been remade of steel and wiring was climbing alone. He wanted to achieve the height of the mountain for surveillance purposes. If he could spot any pursuers, he could perhaps pick them off with the rifle now slung over his shiny metal shoulders. If they were nowhere to be seen, then he could simply set the charges at the top of the mountain, and descend. The mountain had masses of snow that would fall on the slightest concussion from the time bomb he carried in his satchel.

If metal could smile, Chrome's face would have been set in a grin as he climbed. Certainly the man who Chrome once was, the man called Gunter, the man who had been rebuilt from practically nothing, would have smiled. Chrome was sure Killov was right. Rockson somehow would be following. The history of the so-called Doomsday Warrior demanded such foolishly brave action.

Chrome looked around, searching for the right spot. The crevice his electronic scope vision detected halfway up the mountain would do, a small cave-like indentation, just big enough to set the ten liters of explosive in. He set down the carcass and rifle and began the climb using pinions only where needed, relying on the enormous strength of his servomechanism-driven arms to carry him from fingerhold to fingerhold. The lower slope, full of jagged bare-rock outcroppings, was made for a swift climb—at least by an expert such as he.

In an hour's time his steel hands pulled him up and over into the small cave. It was deep enough for Chrome to roll his body into. He unpacked the explosive package and attached the sensing microphone and wires. He did this with speed and efficiency. He was hardly winded by the climb. Chrome exulted in this near-limitless endurance.

Nothing can stop me, nothing can kill me, nothing, he thought with a madman's pride. He attached the end of the hundred and fifty foot rope of nylon braid with a piton he hit deep into the rock, using only his steel fist. He wanted to get down in a hurry, to continue his search-and-destroy mission. He pulled on the rope and made sure it would bear his weight, then he slid down it at a speed that would have burned another's hand. He reached another toehold, steadied himself, and yanked the rope above loose with a tremendous pull. Then he gathered it, inserted another piton in the granite mountain, attached the rope again, and repeated the process. Doing this ten times he made the descent in a mere five minutes.

Satisfied that he had put the explosive at the best possible place along the tremendous icecap of the mountain, he retrieved his rifle and the carcass of the caribou. He would scout west next, and then south. He had his electron binoculars, some raw meat, and the Dragunov rifle. He could last out here for weeks. In a perverse way, he hoped the avalanche *didn't* get them, for he wished to kill Rockson personally. He'd pick off the other Americans when he saw them, but would face Rockson with only his steel-crushing hands as weapons.

The metal slit of a mouth moved up and down. It was a laugh, without sound, without humor. He walked away from the mountain careful not to make a noise, for the charges were set to go off at the sound of a human voice, or a dog's bark, or the tramping of feet.

Chapter 20

After leaving the Ice City, Rockson and his men pushed north into the forbidding area the Eskimos called the Devil's Playground. It was a landscape of twisting canyons and smoking volcanic cones, some hundreds of feet in height. Only the guidance of the Ice City men enabled the party to choose the right path to take through the labyrinth of death. The temperature, by the fifth day out, had dropped to a constant minus forty-five degrees. They still managed to cover more than eighty miles a day, and by the time they reached a frozen lake, Rockson's sextant indicated they had crossed the 64th parallel.

When they reached the middle of the twenty-mile-wide lake there was a sudden piercing howl, a sound to chill the bones of the most hardened Fighter—then another.

A chorus of death filled the air. Rock knew the sound—a wolf pack was after them. The howls were carried by the wind, dozens of wolf voices.

"Quickly," Rock shouted. "Cut right, to the bank

of the lake, into those woods. If we're lucky there will be dry wood there. We'll build a fire to keep them away."

The sleds turned as one on the frozen lake and raced in the moonlight toward the shoreline a mile away. Behind them now, dozens of wolves poured out of the night, their gray pelts glistening in the white-fire moonlight, their intended victims well visible to their night eyes. Like the fires of a predatory sun their hot-coal eyes burned. Thoughts of tender raw meat that they would soon savor in their sharp-toothed jaws made them salivate in streams. They needed food to carry to their young. The wolves were gaining on their prey.

Rockson whipped away at his team, flicking the whip tip against their moon-silhouetted ears. They yelped and pulled harder. He hated to treat them roughly—but they didn't want to be eaten either, he was sure of that. If a shot to their ear tips was what it took to get them moving at top speed, so be it.

Yet the wolves cries grew louder. The Freefighters were losing ground. A glance over Rock's shoulder showed the ghostly images of fast-approaching death on paws. They were less than fifty yards behind now. He unholstered his shotpistol and set it for wide dispersal. But the weapon was no good for such distance. And there was no way any of the men could get their rifles up and fire accurately at this pace.

Rock could dimly see the glint of other shotpistols being pulled out. A shot was fired—McCaughlin's. His sled was furthest back, his dogs being the least able to achieve the needed speed. There was a yelp; Rock saw a furry shape tumble to a halt on the whiteness behind. A good shot!

The wolves spread out now, as if they knew to disperse reduced the risk of more than one wolf getting hit at a time. Rockson was dismayed. He'd hoped that they'd stop to eat the wolf who had fallen. Rock expected that some bloody meat, even of their own kind, would be sufficient to stall their attack. But they were intent on human meat, or dog meat, or a smorgasbord of both.

He sighted as best he could and fired at the nearest wolf. The thing howled and fell, rolling end over end. But again it did nothing to stop the advance of the others. They had spread out in a wide arc that was beginning to encircle the sleds like a vise, even as they flew over the ice. These were no ordinary wolves, Rock realized with a start. They had a strategy, a leader, they could communicate. He noticed a certain rhythm, a certain give-and-take in the seemingly random yelps. The damned things were communicating.

"Men—shout, make noise, keep firing. They're talking wolf lingo to one another. We've got to drown out the commands the lead wolves are giving."

Rock saw what appeared to be one of the leaders, a big brown wolf, catching the moonlight far off to the right. He had to get a good shot at him, but how? As the men continued firing at every opportunity, Rock leapt aboard the sled he had been gliding behind on his skis. His added weight further slowed down the team, but it couldn't be helped.

He crawled forward over the blankets covering the supplies, felt a long frigid object—his Liberator

9mm rifle. He tore off the blankets and pulled the rifle out, switched on its laser sight, checked the clip. He lay belly down. The sled danced and swerved forward, guided by the panicked dogs. Rock swung the light-sensitive scope around the horizon, found the big brown leader wolf. He lined the thing's mad eyes in the crosshairs and squeezed off a full clip of 9mm explosive slugs. He got it. He swung the rifle slowly around again. The laser night sight found another, much closer wolf. It was coming toward Rock from only yards away. Its huge fangs opened far apart, ready to slam shut on human meat.

Rockson turned his attention to this more immediate problem. The devil in gray fur leapt, was suddenly upon him, knocking the wind from him, raking his body with its huge claws, biting. Having no other weapon at hand, he swung the Liberator's stock, used it to slam the drooling jaws from his jugular. The teeth imbedded instead in his right shoulder. Pain shot through him, then numbness. He had no more use of that arm. He slammed the rifle butt again and again into the teeth, but it was an exercise in futility, and the awful realization that the next time the oversized incisors bit into him it might be the end welled up in his soul.

But a solid blow stunned the wolf. Rockson pulled the thing to the side and, dangling precariously half off the speeding sled, threw the creature from him. Half his parka tore from his body, caught in the locked jaws of the monster. The wolf fell away. He was alone again on the sled. But more red eyes were just feet behind; he could hear their labored breathing.

A rifle shot rang out, then another—a whole burst—and the wolves immediately behind his sled tumbled like bloody snowballs. He saw McCaughlin's sled zoom past him. McCaughlin flashed the thumbs-up.

Rockson, who somehow still had his short steel skis locked on, crawled back to the end of his sled and took his old position, hanging on for dear life as he made contact with the rapidly passing ice beneath him. He was nearly jerked off his feet, but held the handle with a steel grip in his good left hand. Somehow he managed not to fall. The full weight of his body gone now, the dogs increased speed. Any second, he half expected one of the huskies' hearts to burst.

Tinglim pulled alongside him, yelling something, whipping his dogs like mad. "We've been separated," he yelled. "Someone's missing!"

Indeed, there were only five sleds now. The wolves suddenly were nowhere to be seen.

A howling chorus of wolves' voices, a cry of victory—Rock knew that's what it was—went out now. The chorus of hell-voices spoke of their triumph. They had a human and six dogs somewhere back there on the bloodstained ice, and they were already tearing their prey apart in their bloody jaws. The wolves had won—this round.

At the roaring fire that night, Rockson sat with his head buried in his hands. Pedersen, good old Pedersen—gone. He had liked the man. It wasn't the way to die, ripped apart by wolves. But then there

197

were few ways to go that were particularly pleasant.

And the death of Pedersen wasn't the only thing troubling the Doomsday Warrior. There was the constant image of Archer. The big lug lay near death—or already dead—back in Ice City. And Rock himself had lost use of his right arm. Farrell, acting the medic again, had made it a sling. The throbbing pain reassured Rock that the arm still was alive, still connected despite the huge teeth wounds. Tinglim rubbed some bear salve in the wounds and the pain diminished. Tinglim told him, as the fire roared its red threat into the icy sky, "There is little danger of infection, wolves are very clean creatures. They don't eat decayed meat, only fresh, warm flesh. And the salve I put on your wounds will knit them closed very very soon. You will see!"

More misfortune—and totally unexpected—found them before dawn. One of the best sled dogs slept too close to the fire. As a big stem cracked and popped in the fire, a hot coal burst out and caught in the dog's pelt. The dog rose yelping and leapt into the woods. It didn't yelp for long. Before anyone could go after it, its sounds were cut off by the snapping jaws of things huge and mean. They couldn't sleep after that, as exhausted as they were.

Dawn came, its fingers of amber light like the hand of a cadaver reaching up for a chance of rebirth. But there was none. Just the barrenness of the dead forest they had camped in: Twisted, gnarled tree trunks and fallen branches, and around it a white barren wasteland stretching seemingly forever.

Rockson felt weary of spirit, not just of body, as he scanned the way ahead. It was so very cold—the belt thermometer said minus thirty. Could Killov still be alive out there? Or was his body sprawled under a dozen wolves, just foul meat. Somehow the bastard always survived. Only last month he'd had Killov in his sights and was about to dispatch the dark one to hell when the fiend pressed a button and rocketed away in an escape module that had snapped shut around his chair.

No, he lives, Rockson thought, I know it. He expects us to give up, to not follow him through this hellish frozen wasteland. But I will follow him to the gate of hell and beyond if I have to, to finish him off. I will stand over his dead body and pump slug after slug into it, make sure he stays dead. Pedersen and many other good men had been lost in the attempt to stop Killov. Their deaths must not be in vain. With Killov dead, the whole world could have a few decent nights' sleep, Russians and Americans alike.

Scheransky took another antimatter meter reading. It indicated that Killov was about four days' hard traveling ahead of them. The Russian major's once plump, but now gaunt face was blistered and cracked from the cold. He had lost all his excess weight, too. He was trembling constantly, ever since Pedersen was lost. "Please, let us go back. This is insane. I can't go on," Scheransky pleaded.

"We go on, buddy," Rock said. "Sorry."

Scheransky threw a fit. "You Americans—you— you—are mad. Crazy. You—you are a suicidal race."

"Maybe," Rock said. "Maybe we are suicidal or maybe we just value freedom more than our lives."

To get on as quickly as possible, Rock decided to cut the loads of the remaining sleds. He began to go through the supplies they carried. What could be dispensed with? There was only one answer: the heavy stoves—four out of five would have to go. Rockson hated to do it, but there was no choice. They moved too dangerously slow.

Food was now a problem too. Pedersen's sled, the one that was lost, had had most of their food supplies on it. So, while the rest of the party remained camped, the three Ice City Eskimos, Ngaicook, Dalmok, and Zebok, strode off through the dead forest with their harpoons and rifles.

It was Zebok who found the first trace of the caribou family a few miles beyond the camp. The Eskimos followed the meandering trail of the three animals—past clump after clump of lichens that had been nibbled to the quick.

The men spread out when Ngaicook's sensitive nose picked up the smell of the caribou.

Each of the Eskimos moved silently, surely, through the snow, careful to stay downwind from the quick creatures. If the caribou caught their scent before they were within range, they would be gone in an instant.

They came at the caribou buck and the two does in a small lichen-filled clearing. They had already decided to kill only the smallest of the three graceful creatures. It would be sufficient for the food requirement, and Eskimos did not kill for sport. They crept quietly to within a hundred feet of the group.

Suddenly the big buck looked up in alarm and began running. Ngaicook opened fire, and an instant later so did the others. The smallest doe fell immediately, dead before she hit the ground. After whispering their apologies in the dead animal's ear, which was the Eskimo custom, they quickly cut all the meat from the animal and headed back toward Rockson and the others.

Jubilant voices shouted out praise for the good hunters. McCaughlin prepared a man-sized caribou steak dinner for all of the men. The rest of the meat was loaded, a bit to each sled, and after the dogs were fed the gristle and fattier parts—and the bones—they were on their way much fortified.

Chapter 21

After three more days of arduous travel, the cold and weary attack team came directly below the enormous volcanic mountain called Mount Draco. It was a mountain that hadn't existed before the earth upheavals that had occurred in the atomic war four generations ago. Its towering twin 21,000-foot summits were loaded with glacial ice.

Rockson had the men stream out their sleds in a long single file as they passed to the west of the sometimes-lost-in-the-clouds peaks. He wanted the group to make as little noise as possible, for there was the danger of an avalanche.

The sleds were nearly beyond the pass and out in the flat snow of the plain again when the lead dog of Tinglim's sled stepped on a sharp rock. He let out a yelp that set the other dogs to barking as if in sympathy.

There was a sharp *crack* far above. The giant mass of glacial ice somewhere in the cloud-covered slope above pulled free and started down.

The Doomsday Warrior thought it had sounded like an explosion.

With a sickening feeling in his stomach, Rockson screamed, *"Mush*—mush, you huskies," and snapped the whip. His sled instantly lurched forward. The cracking above had given way to a rising rumble. It vibrated their sleds. A wall of ice began moving down the slopes above. The sleds behind Rock were losing ground, but he could still hear their panicked yelping dogs. The rumbling, like a thousand freight trains, was overtaking them. Rockson tensed his body as he expected to feel the crushing weight of a million tons of white death smash onto him and his team any second. He snapped the whip again and again as the dogs howled and panted, the rumbling sounds echoing and building louder and louder. It was a race against white death—a race that seemed futile.

The massive cloud of snow dust behind them blotted out the pale Arctic sun; the way grew so dark that he could barely see a thing. The massive death wave towered over them as if their sleds were some tiny insects about to be smashed to bits by the enormous white hammer of a giant.

The dogs pulled like they never had before, nearly bursting their strong canine hearts as the sleds began the climb up a foothill. The mighty masses of volcanic rock beneath the skids of the fleeing sleds shook as if there was an earthquake. Rockson glided on behind the sled, holding the vibrating handles for dear life.

The first of the snow waves struck the far side of the slope the men were on, but was unabated by the rise of terrain. First came the lighter powdery snow. Then came the rocks and ice boulders each the size of a house, smashing into and colliding with one another in one liquid wave. The huge tumbling things plummeted toward the puny creatures who were attempting to elude it.

The two sleds furthest back were enveloped by a fog of white powder that preceded the huge avalanche.

Rock put his sleds on a diagonal course—up the slope to the left. The sled strained, nearly turning over in its course. If they could reach even another hundred feet up the gently rolling hill, there was the slim chance the roaring avalanche would just pass them by, heading down the valley.

Looking back to make sure his men saw his move, Rock saw the awesome thousand-foot-high wall of snow moving forward. It looked like a whole planet was rolling at them. Rockson was enveloped in the white powder mist.

The avalanche was now a living thing, an evil entity determined to snuff out the intruders in its cold domain. The wall of ice and snow hollowed itself into one huge breakerlike wave.

Rockson searched for some cover. The roiling white powdery mist parted at that moment. *There!* To his left, barely visible between two boulders, was a blue darkness in the side of the snowslope. It looked like an ice cave. If they could only reach it . . .

Rather than screaming back to the men behind him, for his voice would be lost, the best thing Rockson could do was head there himself. He turned the team, nearly whipping the ears off the lead dogs to push them to the top speed possible. The Doomsday Warrior's sled sped past the misshapen ice boulder, plunged into the blue-black darkness of the cave.

He could see nothing, but the echoing yips of his dogs and the icy ground grating under the sled told him they were still moving forward at great velocity. He pulled the flashlight out of his sealskin parka, lit it, and saw the precipice ahead—a fall into a nearly bottomless steaming abyss. He yanked back hard, nearly beheading the dogs who tumbled in a heap, bringing the sled to an abrupt stop. Suddenly he heard shouts, more dog yelps behind him. One after the other, the sleds had followed him into the ice cave.

They all heard the tremendous concussion of the snowmass hitting the mouth of the cave, the snowmass stopped short, though sealing them inside. Rock got off the sled and ran back to see who the hell had made it and who was buried forever beneath a million tons of ice.

Chen, Robinson, Detroit, McCaughlin, Tinglim, Scheransky, and himself were in. The Eskimo guides too had made it—miraculous.

They sat down, exhausted, in the lights of several flashlights, too exhausted to speak. After several minutes of stunned silence, Rockson rallied them to begin digging out. They whittled away at the snowmass with their shovels, depositing the snow in the steaming pit. "We don't know," confided Rockson, "how deep we're buried. I've noticed that the temperature is rising. The volcanic steam will make this cave our watery tomb. We must dig as hard and fast as we can."

After hours of exhausting digging, using the same method of cutting out blocks of ice that they had used to build the emergency igloo, they had accomplished little. The men were starting to breathe with difficulty. The air was filled with hot steam and, Rock suspected, sulphur gases from the abyss at the far end of the cave. It was choking them. The walls of the ice cave were melting, drips became rivulets of running water.

Soaked, they continued to frantically dig, passing the ice blocks to be dumped in the abyss.

Rockson wondered how long they could go on. The desperate team was near their last breaths—when suddenly there was a *whoosh* and a blast of frigid air.

They had reached the outside world!

They made sure their dogs and sleds were okay and then set off again. Rockson and the others were silent. The sun, which had been edging over the horizon, sank. The northern lights came on like a neon sign sending blue-green curtains across the starlit sky.

Rockson realized it hadn't been sheer luck that he had found the ice cave that had saved them. It had been timing. If he hadn't been at that precise place on the slope at the exact moment when the ice cave was visible through the white mists, they would have all perished. Could the Ice Shaman's delaying tactics have arranged it all? He would never know for sure.

On and on they plunged into the near-endless

darkness of the forbidding northlands. After a brief rest stop, they spent the next twelve hours speeding across an enormous flat expanse. It grew colder by the hour. It was down to almost minus forty degrees and was still dropping by the time they joined together three tents and crawled into the shelter. They huddled close to the seal-oil heater that was their life-giver. But they were short of precious fuel and it had to be used sparingly.

Chen and McCaughlin had frostbitten feet. Rockson was deeply worried about them, but nothing could be done except to try to keep the flesh as warm as possible and move the injured tissue as much as possible to keep the blood circulating. Tinglim brought one dog—a precious lead dog that was whining a lot—into the cramped quarters. The big brownish husky had scarred feet. Rockson had a look. The pads of the dog's feet were badly torn.

Rock greased its feet with fat cut from wolf meat. Tinglim lashed soft sealskin on the pads of the dog.

Rockson had never even thought of such a thing, dog boots. He was sure the dog would rip the makeshift shoes off, but the big gentle husky hunkered down and put its head on Rock's lap. "They won't accept shoes until they are actually bleeding," Tinglim said. "Then they see the light. Necessity is the mother of acceptance."

Rockson nodded. Perhaps, with Tinglim's resourcefulness, they would yet win out against the northern hell.

They slept for six hours then moved on.

Chapter 22

Rockson took a sextant reading on the low sun. They were five miles from the Arctic Circle. Scheransky set up the antimeter tracker. He excitedly reported to a numbed-cold Rockson that the readings indicated the five missiles were less than six miles away. Killov hadn't moved since their last reading.

Rockson looked north through the snow flurries at the rolling hills of tundra ahead of them. Killov. At last.

Rockson wondered if Killov was making camp for a few hours or had set up what would be his launch base. He suspected the latter. The mad colonel didn't have to go any further. He was at the right latitude now, the Arctic Circle, to threaten Moscow, Colorado, the whole damned world!

The date was December 22, the date of the winter solstice. At this extreme altitude, the sun wouldn't come up again for three months. Rock and his attack force would have the first *Black Day*, total darkness on their side, when they attacked. *Today*, at noon!

They set off on skis, moving quickly over the rolling terrain. The weather was good and they could steer by the faint light of the stars.

A few miles on, Rock's calculations were proven correct. They had effected the overland shortcut and intersected the Alaskan Highway. They saw it when they crested a tundra hillock—snow-covered, a long smooth roadway stretching back toward the southwest.

Detroit excitedly pointed. "Look, there are tire tracks from large vehicles in the snow."

The Freefighters skied down to the roadway, and Rock inspected the big tracks more closely.

"I'd say these were made less than a day or two ago."

Rock scanned the horizon on the north with his electron binoculars. *There!* At the side of the road some miles up—a row of structures. Killov's base, alongside the highway. "Let's get up the hill again, under better cover behind those rocks," the commander ordered, "and take a look from there."

A scan of the base with the high-power light-amplification lenses showed that the KGB force were busy as bees, constructing quonset-type buildings, guard towers, and the like. There were lots of troops down there, possibly a hundred. "The trailer with the large radio antenna jutting from it must be Killov's headquarters," Rock said. "It's right in the middle of the base." The three-hundred-meter-wide base was surrounded by double razor-wire coils ten feet high. There were electric wires running to the coils.

Rock wondered for a while what the KGBers were

doing in their heavy Arctic work overalls out beyond the camp. Rock focused in on the workers. They were smoothing out the bumpy ground, making it flat. Were they completing a rough airstrip? Rock wondered. It looked like it.

"We have no time to lose," Rock said. "God knows, he's expecting planes—they'd be very unwelcome company for us. Once Killov has completely fortified and brought in additional troops by air, we may not be able to stop him."

Further scanning showed the trucks—ten of them—that had carried the troops, and five large balloon-tired vehicles, presumably the ones that had carried the missiles. But these missile trucks no longer carried anything. Rock scanned the camp again. Those corrugated-metal quonset huts, they were really missile bunkers. Five of them, each fifty feet long by twenty wide. Scheransky said, "See the hinges at one side of the roof of each of the huts? They open up like a cigar box. The missile pops up on its launcher arm, and is fired. Those are the standard field bunkers for the missiles. The launch crew, four men to each missile, stay inside the building—until launch, of course, which requires a four-minute countdown."

Tinglim put down his binoculars, and smiled broadly. "I might have good news. Remember the oil shortages of the twentieth century? How a great pipeline was built by you Americans through Alaska and through part of the Yukon to carry oil from the north southward?"

"Yes. What's that got to do with attacking Killov?"

"Rockson, when you again scan with your

binoculars, don't fail to notice the slight bump in the terrain. It cuts diagonally through the compound, difficult to see at first. That bump, if I am not mistaken, is the covered-up pipe of your ancestors, Rockson—empty, I hope." Tinglim fairly beamed.

Rock took another look. When he crawled back down he said, "If it is the old pipeline, it used to be mostly aboveground, as I recall from the history books. So someplace back to the south it must still break the surface. There's no way of telling, though. And a lot of it could have collapsed. But we'll give it a try. I think I remember reading it was big enough to walk through. Chen, we still have the cutting torches, don't we?"

"Yes," Chen assured the Doomsday Warrior. Chen was in charge of the remaining stores. "No food left, no heating oil, but thank God, we managed to hold onto the torches."

"Then we'll use the pipeline as a highway right into the camp. It's probably very close to the surface there—hence the bump. Killov has no reason to believe he was pursued. We have the element of surprise. They think they are protected well by their razor-wire electric barriers."

"There is a storm brewing in the east. It will bring a good blow and lots of snow for cover in a few hours," Tinglim added.

"Detroit," the Doomsday Warrior ordered, "I want you to equip five of us with stun grenades. We don't want a big explosion near those missiles. And you, Scheransky, you know that Killov is here this far north because he wants to be in range of Moscow. We have to defuse those missiles. There can't be any mistakes. Or boom, there goes Borsht-town. Do you understand? Not to mention my own city, which is still in range."

"My wife is in Moscow—my children go to school there. There will be no mistakes, Rockson, I promise you that," said the trek-hardened major.

They made good time despite a gathering snowstorm. Soon they reached the gigantic rusty pipe, jutting out of the tundra. It was perhaps eight feet in diameter. It looked solid enough.

"It's true, there it is," Rock said, half in disbelief.

"The northern gods have provided our salvation," Tinglim said. "And they have provided us a storm to hide the noise when we cut out of the pipe in Killov's camp."

"Let's get to work, men," Rock ordered.

They broke out torches and set about cutting a man-sized hole in the pipe. Rock winced when the big piece fell out. He half expected crude oil to ooze out, but the pipe was empty, if somewhat crudded up and smelly inside. It had been, after all, a hundred years or more since it had functioned. The twentieth century steel alloy had held up pretty well. He played the light down the seemingly endless interior. It looked like it hadn't collapsed anywhere. McCaughlin hefted the antimatter meter in on his huge shoulders. They needed the heavy piece of equipment to tell them when they were closest to the missiles. It was set to ping at the highest concentration of anitmatter radiation.

When they were all safely in the shelter of the eight-foot-wide oil pipe, the men huddled around Scheransky who opened the diagram of the deadly missile. Rockson played his flashlight beam onto the diagram.

Rock said, "There won't be time for Scheransky to defuse all five missiles. The major will instruct us *all* on how to do it." The major nodded. He looked shaky and pale, Rock thought.

For a precious half-hour, Scheransky explained. Detroit, McCaughlin, Chen, Farrell, and Rockson caught on, but the three Eskimo guides stared in bewilderment. The instructions brought a blank expression to Tinglim's face too. He couldn't fathom it either. Rock decided then and there that there would be five 2-man teams. "One man protects, while the other works on the missile. We use stun grenades to knock out the bunker crews. The grenades won't cause enough shock to blow the missiles up.

"Now, the major has shown you how to open the missiles' wiring sections—each missile is identical—and install the red boxes, the 'antimatter drains' as Scheransky calls them . . ."

Rockson set up each two-man team: Farrell and Dalmok, McCaughlin and Zebok, Chen and Ngai-cook, Detroit and Tinglim. He and Scheransky were the fifth team. If any other team didn't make it, either one of them could rush to finish their job. They started walking in the pipe. Each had a Liberator, enough ammo for a few minutes of fire-fight. Their shotpistols were nearly empty. Ten cold and tired men against hundreds of fanatical KGB Commandos. Not good odds. But Rockson had faced odds nearly as bad in the past and survived.

Scheransky was a little weak-kneed at the idea of

the unfair odds, and had to be encouraged along the interior of the pipe.

It took an hour and a half of claustrophobic trekking down the pipeline before the antimatter meter pinged once.

"We are there," Scheransky whispered.

"This is it," Rockson said. "Finally. What time is it?"

"Eleven A.M., hereabouts," said Chen, checking his all-weather chronometer.

"Give it another hour," suggested Tinglim. "By then the storm should be at its maximum." Rockson nodded.

They sat there, as tense as they had ever been in their lives. At noon, on Rock's order, Chen started cutting through. It didn't take long before a rolling mess of tundra mixed with snow came tumbling in, nearly half burying them. But the flow quickly stopped. They could see the glow of a searchlight. They were through. The howling winds had covered their cutting noise.

A fierce storm—ice and snow, frigid wind—was blasting across the frozen land, making for a near white-out condition. The searchlight that lit the camp merely reflected off the milky swirling snow. Rockson whispered, "Let the searchlight alone unless we're detected. Once the shooting starts, knock it out." They listened for a while. Not a KGBer stirred in the camp, but the men working on the runway several hundred feet away were making their own noise banging down the hard tundra.

Rockson and the others clawed up into the frozen camp, into the numbing cold of the "Black Day."

215

Each man knew exactly what he was supposed to do.

Rock and Scheransky made the first run from the hole, right after the beam of the searchlight swept past. They made a dash for the closest bunker. They hit the snow ten feet from the bunker door and watched the four other teams make their own runs to the other bunkers. In seconds they were all in place. Rock flicked his flashlight for the others to proceed. Their flashlights flicked back.

Rock rose, pushing Scheransky forward. They ran right up to the bunker door. A light was coming through a crack in the metal doorway. They heard laughing.

"Here goes nothing," Rock whispered. He tried the door; it wasn't locked. Rock kicked open the door and threw the stun pineapple in, pushed Scheransky down and to the side in the snow.

Whumppp!

The two attackers entered the smoking interior, stepping over four bodies. Scheransky froze. Rock shook him. "Scheransky—over there, isn't that the missile? Get to it, man!" The major snapped out of it, rushed forward with his red deactivator box and got to work. Rockson stripped off his parka and put on the least-messy Red uniform coat.

Rockson opened the door of the bunker a foot and emptied his Liberator at a squad of Reds caught in their own searchlight's beam. He saw other running shapes out there in the strobelike flashes of gunfire— two of them were carrying something that looked like a mortar. "Hurry!" Rock screamed at Scheransky. "Hurry!"

"I *am* hurrying!" Scheransky screamed back.

Rockson snatched up a Kalishnikov rifle and continued firing in full auto, slashing the air, waving the gun like a wand in front of him, conjuring death. He succeeded in a few lucky shots, heard the crunches as the KGBers fell in front of him, lifeless eyes staring accusingly at him, blood trickling from noses and mouths onto the mauled snow.

Scheransky was dripping cold sweat as he carefully placed the Phillips screwdriver into the first screwhead and loosened it. He knew he'd do it right, but Detroit, Chen, McCaughlin, and Farrell were doing the same thing with very little instruction in the other bunkers. If any one of them made a mistake, they'd *all* be vaporized instantly, along with two hundred and fifty square miles of Arctic wasteland. The major loosened the second screw. Then, with a solid grip on both screws, he pulled them out simultaneously. He removed the cover exposing the wiring, took the red box, and jammed it into place.

"Done!" he yelled triumphantly.

"Let's go!" Rock screamed back.

Rock and Scheransky scrambled out of a side window. When the beam of the searchlight had passed, they ran like jack rabbits out into the drifting snow, back toward their rendezvous with the others—the pipe hole. Seconds after they dove into the cover of the broken-open pipe, the beam of the searchlight passed again, followed by fierce submachine-gun fire. From their vantage point, they could see mortar shells kicking up snow near the bunkers. The fools would get them all killed! Seconds stretched to hours, minutes stretched to eternity, as they waited for the other Freefighters.

217

Detroit came in next, diving in with Tinglim, closely followed by Chen and Ngaicook. A bear of a man came running through the night. It was McCaughlin. Alone. As they pulled his great hulk into the pipe hole, he gasped, "They got Zebok—Farrell and Dalmok too. I saw them lying in the snow outside the fifth bunker."

"Did they defuse the missile?" asked Rock.

"I don't know," McCaughlin answered.

"Scheransky, you come with me," Rock ordered. The rest of you, cover us; and for God's sake, get that searchlight and that mortar crew."

Colonel Killov had been watching the video he had made of the torture of the wandering Eskimo boy they had captured. Suddenly there was shooting, explosions. He ran to the window. The sweeping searchlight silhouetted running figures. He saw bursts of flame from many rifles. Tracer bullets crisscrossed the darkness. There were attackers— many attackers out there. It would take a force of hundreds of commandos to break the camp's perimeter defenses.

As Killov watched wide-eyed, the huge floodlight went out—hit no doubt by enemy bullets. The firing continued, even more wildly. He ran to the P.A.

Killov's voice, cold and thin, but very loud, came over the loudspeaker. *"Fools!* Stop shooting at everything that moves. Turn on the vehicles' headlights. *See* what you are doing. Beware of damaging the missiles."

Rockson and Scheransky took advantage of the

cease-fire order to rush for cover behind some crates.

Following Killov's orders, the KGBers began turning on their headlights. The Freefighters knew what to do. They started shooting them out immediately from their positions as Rock fired from behind his crates. In a matter of moments the lights had been shot out again. Rock and Scheransky had to get the last bunker. They could see it strobed in the light of sporadic submachine-gun fire—fifty yards away.

Killov pressed the intercom buttons to contact all the missile bunkers. Only one bunker answered—the fifth. "We are under attack!" a hoarse voice screamed in reply to the buzzer.

"Fire the missile, you fool, fire the missile!" Killov yelled. "Do it immediately, it's already target-programmed."

"But—but we are in here *with* the missile. We will be killed by the launch flame!"

"Fire the missile on a sixty-second countdown. That should be enough time for you to make a run for it."

"Missile will be fired," the terrified voice replied.

Killov quickly got on the shortwave accessing the channel for Kamchatka Island. The radioman at the Siberian base answered his call immediately. Killov's special channel was monitored twenty-four hours a day. The colonel screamed, "This is Killov, get me General Sirkovnak!"

There was a slight pause, then Sirkovnak's gruff voice came in on the shortwave. "Killov! You are alive? Where are you?"

"I am in the Yukon. Zero in on my broadcast. I have constructed a short runway. Send a rescue jet right away," Killov commanded. "A fast short-takeoff-and-landing plane. My base is under attack."

Sirkovnak's strained voice replied, "I cannot. Vassily has given orders that you are a traitor and that anyone helping you will be executed."

Killov played his last card: "If the rescue plane is not here in twenty minutes, I will inform Vassily that you were part of my 'Doctors' Plot' to kill him. As a matter of fact, you are the last conspirator yet alive. Send two planes: one to land and pick me up, one to fly escort. Do you understand what I say, you fool? Unless that plane picks me up—"

"They will be sent, Excellency! Two of my fastest jets. Twenty minutes at the most."

Wham. A projectile of some sort hit the trailer. Killov fell over on his side, pieces of the trailer's metal walls imbedded in his skin. But he was alive. All he could hear was a ringing in his ears. He staggered to his closet, put on a parka, ran out through the hole that had appeared in the side of the trailer. He ran for his life as tracer bullets lit up the air behind him.

Then he heard a rumble, saw the missile rising on its column of flame. The bunker crew had obeyed his order. He threw up his arms and laughed. Death, megadeath, for Century City.

Chapter 23

Rock watched the deadly missile roar aloft with a despair he had never felt before in his life. *There goes the whole ballgame*, he thought. *I've lost*. He desperately directed his 9mm Liberator rifle fire up at the ascending thing, but it climbed too fast. It headed away. In a matter of seconds, the swift cruise missile was out of range—and he realized it was heading *south*, toward the U.S., not toward the Soviet Union.

His men were still engaged in a deadly fire-fight with overwhelming KGB forces. But for what purpose now?

"Withdraw," he yelled. "Withdraw. There's no reason to stick around now, get to the pipe—get the hell out of here." He was about to do the same when he saw a figure running out of the trailer—Killov. He pulled up his electron binoculars and leapt behind a dune of bloodstained snow, adjusted them—*yes!* A lone black-clad figure, running. *Killov*. The bastard was getting away, heading toward the runway. Killov must have a plane coming in.

Rock abandoned his effort to leave the hellish killing field. He had to catch Killov. Had to wring his scrawny neck. At least that would be something. It was two hundred yards to the airstrip. Stumbling over dead KGBers, he zigzagged, avoiding a trail of bullets, tear-assing after the shadowy figure. Rock was determined not to lose the man. He dove headfirst over several snowy moguls and in quick time made it to the tarmac runway; he'd cut off Killov. Rockson pulled his shotpistol up to the ready and waited, concealed by a pile of construction supplies at the edge of the snow-blown tarmac.

A shape, a huge *shape*, silhouetted against the raging fires back in the camp, confronted him. It wasn't human, that was certain. Its half-torn-away uniform revealed glistening chrome and steel parts. It was seven feet tall if an inch. And it stepped out in front of Rockson and blocked his way. The thing, in a frightening metallic voice, uttered three words, "You die here."

"Not today," Rock said emphatically. He didn't know who—or rather *what*—the man-machine was, but he had no time to play "animal, vegetable, or mineral." He opened up with his shotpistol, firing directly into his opposer's chest. Bullets ricocheted off metal. Nothing else. The man-machine just stood there.

Its gleaming chrome steel chest was undamaged, though stripped of cloth by the X pattern of shot pellets. The thing should have been blasted to bits, but it stood.

"I said, you die here, Rockson," said the slit mouth.

Rock asked, "Who are you? How do you know my name?"

"You killed me, Rockson, yet I live . . ."

"Don't speak in riddles, pal, who are you?"

"Gunter used to be my name. You killed me in the battle of Forrester Valley. You blew me apart with a huge projectile. But I was re-created, Rockson, and now I am a superior being. They call me Chrome, because of all my shiny metal. I am invincible. You die here."

"Gunter! The Nazi!"

"Yes, Rockson. A miracle of KGB science, is it not? I am a cyborg. Part human, mostly robot. Enough talk, now you die."

Rockson had no time to think about it, the horror was coming at him again.

Rockson caught a glimpse of Killov, silhouetted briefly in the fire from the camp. Damned! The man had reached the opposite side of the runway—and he was crouching there now, gleefully watching the standoff between Rockson and Chrome. Rock heard Killov shout triumphantly, "My rescue jet will soon be here, but I have a ringside seat while I wait to watch your death, Rockson. Please don't kill him too fast, Chrome, amuse me until I must go."

"I will amuse," said Chrome's booming voice. "Watch."

Rock fired again, spraying the giant gleaming metal thing with the rest of his cartridges, hitting every part of the thing's body. Nothing. It smiled. "Time to die, Rockson."

Rock threw the gun down and dove toward something he saw jammed into the tundra a few feet away— a substitute weapon, of a sort. He grabbed the handle of the thing. It was a pneumo-pick—a pick of the type you used to dig up concrete, powered by a small fuel cell in the handle. When used, the tip of the pick glowed with white heat. The tool was designed to vibrate and burn its way deep into the ground. Surely it could do some damage to this junkheap confronting him.

Rock hefted the big pick in his hand. Chrome just stood there, waiting. Rock wondered if Chrome might be slow. *Maybe.* In that case, he could just run around the metal man—no use fighting if he could just dodge the damned monster. He had to get Killov.

Chrome moved toward the Doomsday Warrior through the swirling blur of snow that continued to pile up around them. Rockson hefted the pneumo-pick. He braced it against his forearm, knowing that to do any real damage to his enemy he would have to strike quick, hard, and often.

"Give up, human." The grating mechanical voice came from Chrome's head. "You cannot beat me. No human can. Do you not understand?" His slit mouth rose and fell, a poor facsimile of real lips.

Rockson swung the pick with all his might at the monster's chest.

Despite the red-hot electrical energy biting out of the delivery end of the pick, and the fury with which it was delivered, the tool did little damage to the cyborg. He swung again. The best Rockson was able to do was keep the metal man off balance. Every time Chrome would reach for Rockson, the man would dodge back a step and then push in again, slamming the business end of the pick up against the shielded chestplate—but only managing to scratch the surface and knock his opponent back a step or two.

"You waste your time, human. Come to me, come and die."

The cyborg ground his left heel against a rock protruding from the ground. It crumbled to dust. He moved forward, more rapidly. "I will squeeze you into pulp," he intoned metallically.

Rockson saw some patches of ice, and moved in that direction. Maybe Tinman would slip on the ice.

Rockson dodged the wildly grasping metal arms and thudded the business end of the pick against Chrome's shoulder. But the cyborg braced, and the weight of the attack did not move him, even though his right foot was on ice.

Chrome reached forward with incredible speed, and caught Rockson's left shoulder. Digging in, he forced the man into screaming agony. The metal fingers pressed bones, muscles, and nerves together, bugging Rockson's eyes with pain. The pick slipped from his fingers, bouncing twice and stopping in the snow with a sizzle several feet away. Rockson did not care. The pain tearing through his shoulder was too immediate, too real, to allow him to worry about anything else.

Chrome maintained an even pressure, his fingers never tiring. He did not break the skin, not yet. It would be too soon. He wanted to tear the puny human's shoulder, crush the clavicle and its surrounding deltoid muscles. But that would all be too easy—there would be no fun in that for Colonel Killov, who had instructed Chrome to kill Rockson slowly.

Rockson's mind swam through the pain clogging his system, looking for a way out of his situation. Automatically his jerking body thrashed out at Chrome. His right fist struck again and again at the cyborg, became numb. His feet kicked repeatedly. He knew none of this could help him, though. Rock tried to think, to see a real way out. His breath came in wild gasps, the Arctic air tore at his throat as he sucked each lungful in and out, his brain fought against the agony lancing his body. Finally he saw his only chance to break the hold his enemy had on him, and put himself back in the ball game as a player, and not just a memory.

"Shall I kill you now, Human Rockson?"

"Maybe," choked Rockson through the pain, "maybe *not* just fuckin' yet, pal." He put his plan into action.

He hooked his left foot behind the cyborg's right and jerked with all his remaining strength, pulling the metal man's foot across the sheet of ice, causing him to lose his balance. The pair teetered for a second, and then went crashing down, slipping across the landscape. The hold on Rockson's shoulder loosened. The metal fingers closed only on torn fabric.

The instant Chrome fell, Rock pulled away, rolling across the ground away from the cyborg. The pain throbbing throughout his body lashed at him, trying to force him to give up. And before he had even stopped rolling, Chrome was on his feet, circling the ice to finish Rockson off.

Rock dove across the ice patch, sliding to the pneumo-pick, and grabbed it with his right hand.

Rockson made to stand, but without thinking began to push up with his left hand. The pain shot through him again, dropping him on his stomach. He bit his tongue as his head hit the frozen ground. Through a veil of wildly dancing lights, Rockson could see Chrome coming around again for him.

"Get up, human. Get up so I can tear your fingers off and feed them to you, one bloody little human lump at a time."

Rock scrambled to his feet. "I doubt it, Tin Man," he said with weakening bravado.

Tin Man, Tin Man . . . What was there *about* the Tin Man in *The Wizard of Oz?* Rock remembered: His joints got rusty—so he couldn't move. Well, Rock couldn't make Chrome's joints rusty, but he *could* try the pneumo-pick against Chrome's joints. Maybe he could disable Chrome even if he couldn't kill him. Maybe he could break his joints, if not his body. Rockson swung his pneumo-pick and drove it into Chrome's left knee-joint with all the force he had. Sparks flew from the knee-joint; the cyborg took several involuntary steps back and then fell to his knees.

"Gotcha, you bastard." Rock yelled, encouraged for the first time.

Pressing his advantage, Rockson drove the pick forward again and again, guided only occasionally by the flashes of fire from the camp. Rockson varied his attack this time.

Rockson tried every joint he could find, swinging at the waist, the knees, the flap plating over the ribs, though his blows were weakened by the fact that his right arm helped but little—but nothing gave. By now Chrome's uniform was in shreds, only flapping tatters remained. The pick scorched half a dozen of the cyborg's joints. But though half afire, Chrome stood up. No joint had broken.

Rock backed off, overturned a dozen oil canisters, then dodged around the pile. Chrome stopped short, trying to guess at the man's plan; hesitation set in. Rockson might be trying to sneak off around the other side of the debris so that he could get to Killov, shielded by the darkness. Chrome's yellow computer eyes searched the area. Negative. Rockson was still behind the big drums. The cyborg began circling them the other way. It was at the instant that Chrome turned his back that Rockson made his move. Coming back the same way he had begun circling the debris, Rockson drove the pneumo-pick into the back of Chrome's left knee. Chrome fell on his chest, shaking the tundra, sparks flying from damaged circuitry where Rockson's weapon had impacted.

Rock struck again, at the rear of his other knee. Chrome crawled forward at tremendous speed on his hands and knees, dragging himself out of the pneumo-pick's range to keep Rockson from hitting again. Rockson thought he was winning, but the damage had been less than the spectacular sparking indicated. Chrome suddenly kicked back, catching Rockson in the legs. Chrome regained his feet before the Doomsday Warrior actually hit the ground. Spinning quickly, he moved to finish Rockson off.

Rockson rolled over, bringing the pneumo-pick up in front of him to ward off the cyborg. Chrome rushed past where the Doomsday Warrior had just been and Rockson thrust the pick upward, catching it in a chink of the armored plating over the cyborg's left elbow-joint. As Chrome made to pull back, Rockson jammed the pick in deeper, and then twisted to the left, rolling away from the metal man, jamming the electric cutting edge of the tool into the cyborg's elbow-joint. More sparks.

The two separated and regained their feet. Rockson held onto the pick, gasping for air. His shoulder was throbbing, his vision blurring from the pain. Chrome held his arm up for his own inspection. The fingers and wrist would not respond, their pulleys snapped. From the elbow down, the arm had been rendered useless. He had been hurt!

"Very good, human. Very efficient. You have damaged me. I never thought to see the day." The metallic voice drifted slightly, as if Chrome was having trouble believing his injury had actually happened.

"Look at this," said the cyborg, swinging his ruined arm freely in the wind. "It does not hurt. I cannot be hurt."

Chrome moved forward solidly, swiftly, his one good arm reaching, searching under those cold, yellow computer eyes.

Rockson stepped back, but could not dodge the running onslaught of the metal man. He tried to bring the pneumo-pick to bear again on his foe, but it was torn from his hands. Chrome fingered it in his still-operational hand, twirling the heavy tool as if it were a baton.

"This was your salvation, human. Your only hope." The cyborg snapped it, threw the pick to the ground behind him. "Now you have no hope."

Rockson leapt at Chrome, in a feet-forward drop-kick, throwing all his weight against the metal man. Chrome took a step backward on impact. Rockson fell sickly off to one side. Chrome picked him up by the collar like a rag doll and hurled Rock one-handed into a pile of trash. Rockson slammed against machine parts and shards of broken plastic that grated beneath him as he made to stand. Blood filled his mouth, flowing from the spot where he had again bitten his tongue on impact. Dazed, he stumbled down the heap, looking for anything he might use against the cyborg. He wouldn't give up, he wouldn't sink into oblivion without one more try. But Chrome was already there.

Reaching out, Chrome caught hold of Rockson's previously injured shoulder and again squeezed. Rockson screamed aloud, bleating against the merciless pressure. He slammed his hands and feet against the cyborg's body as it lifted him into the air, but to no avail. The metal man allowed it, welcomed the blows. Now that he knew beyond a shadow of a doubt that he was the victor, he enjoyed Rockson's feeble attempts to do him damage. He turned to face Killov. "Shall I kill him now?" he asked. Chrome could hear Killov's reply, almost lost in the wind: "Yes, kill Rockson."

Rockson could fight no longer. The pain overtook him; he screamed into the darkness in mindless fury. Forgetting Killov, even Chrome, he screamed an animal wail of rage, cursing his pain with sound and bellowing, unable to form words or even think. The cyborg dropped him at its feet.

"Pitiful meat-thing," it began. "You lay in the dirt

screaming with your eyes filled with water. I will stomp you like a bug."

Rock wasn't listening. He inched to the side. He had spotted a cable just a few feet away sticking from the debris. Maybe it could be used as a whip or something. Chrome seemed to have some unexpected difficulty lifting his foot. One of the knee-joints Rock attacked had balked.

Rockson suddenly felt that strange "mutant's luck" feeling in his gut—the same feeling that had guided him in many times of crisis. With his last energy he wildly rolled to the side. Chrome's metal foot stomped the ground where Rock's head had been. But Rock's searching hand found something, the cable. He gripped the cable in both hands and, ignoring the pain, got into a crouch and pulled, freeing it from the mound, only to find a heavy block-and-tackle-style pulley dangling on the end of it. Grinning, Rockson staggered to his feet, starting to swing the thing over his head.

"Okay. Now for Round Three."

Some distance away, Killov squinted to see Chrome and Rockson. Did Chrome throw Rockson down and stomp him? It looked like that. Chrome was an indestructible killing machine, and Rockson was mere flesh and blood, but still he had worried that the mechanical man might not be able to stop Rockson. Damned, the fires back at the camp had died, there were no strobes of light to see anything at all. But all of a sudden there was a light from the sky.

Rockson was running through the snow, doing something with his hands, waving them over his head—no, spinning something. He was attacking

Chrome! With a new weapon. Killov couldn't believe that Rockson was still alive, let alone still fighting. Where the hell was his rescue jet? Killov scanned the sky, fearful now. There—that light. Was that the jet?

Rockson rapidly closed the distance between himself and his metal enemy. He still had a shot at doing some damage. Counting on his luck, Rock spun the heavy pulley hard till it made a *whooshing* noise. He closed on Chrome, bouncing the spinning heavy pulley off the cyborg's good arm. The metal man twisted from the impact and Rockson struck again, crashing the bludgeon against the shining eyes turning toward him. The pulley sent sparks flying into the night from the cyborg's right eye, only to be pulled away and then used again for the same duty. The pulley-and-cable attack was swifter than the one he could mount with the pneumo-pick.

Rockson attacked over and over, raining weighted blows on the metal man's face, trying to get the eyes protected by Chrome's good hand. His shoulder was just pure agony, but he ignored it. Rockson kept him at bay with the cable and pulley, and the eyes started sparking, then flames shot from them. But the cyborg reached out quickly and caught the end of the cable with his good hand. Rockson was instantly jerked from his feet. Ripping the cable out of the human's hands, Chrome snipped the pulley loose with his slicing fingers and then threw it at his enemy, missing Rockson's head by less than an inch. Rockson was halfway to his feet when the cyborg advanced like a boxer and swung, bringing his fist into Rockson's side. *Cracking noises—sharp pain.* Rock fell, rolled coughing phlegm and blood out.

The blow had been too quick, too rapid. The pain knifing through his side was unbearable. Chrome stalked him, carefully, metal feet digging into the snow.

"Rockson!" he shouted. "Rockson." His head turned from side to side.

Rock lay still, panting, not able to move. He had escaped the grasp of the cyborg, only to find he could do little more than crawl. He waited for the moment when Chrome would end his life. Perhaps the metal man would kick him to death, or crush his head in his big hand. This was it.

But the cyborg walked right by him! He can't see me. I've damaged his eyes! Rockson realized.

Rockson silently got to his feet, keeping his eyes on Chrome. The metal man turned, inadvertently showing his foe what had happened: The pulley had crushed the metal grids over Chrome's eyes. Although he was able to guide himself with his internal-movement radar, he could not distinguish one immobile object from another. As the cyborg rushed from one oil drum to another, crushing them, Rockson laughed to himself.

Rockson touched his ribs; the slight touch made him gasp. Chrome turned at the sound. Crossing half the thirty-foot distance between himself and Rockson, he listened intently for any more sounds the man might make. Rockson began inching left. The cyborg followed, probably hearing his footsteps.

Rockson found another of the oil drums. He kicked it over, sending it rolling at Chrome. The metal man tried to stop it with his good hand, but slipped on the ice he couldn't see below his feet, and was knocked down on his back. Standing up quickly, he scanned again for sounds.

Rockson carefully climbed up a mound of debris hoping the cyborg's radar didn't scan *up*. But it was the wrong move. The cyborg's head tilted up when Rock dislodged something. It started climbing, sure-footed, swiftly. Rock was some thirty feet above the metal man. He looked in vain for some weapon the snow-covered trash might yield up to him. The only thing he had left to throw at Chrome was his own body. Where should he aim his steel heels—where? Then he had it in a flash. Chrome had human arrogance, human cruelty—he had a human *brain*. And a brain is connected to a body by the spine—at the back of the neck!

Well, *why not?*

Bracing himself, Rockson tried to judge the distance between himself and the cyborg, then hurtled downward at his foe feet first.

Chrome picked up the movement above him, but dodged too late. Rockson's steel-heeled boots struck the cyborg at the junction of neck and spine, snapping the joints that held the armor there in place. Something happened; the metal man's mouth opened but made no sound. He jerked, his good arm thrashed around, uncontrolled. Chrome even hit himself with it.

Rockson fell heavily to the ground, rolling as best he could with the blow to protect his shattered ribs. He looked back at the teetering giant, expecting him to turn and finish him finally. There was a *whooshing* sound above, a bright light—a plane!

Red sparks shot from the back of Chrome's head,

lighting the night. As the wind drove more of the flying snow into the crack, the electrical reactions grew greater until, finally, the cyborg toppled to the ground. At first he flopped wildly, but finally Chrome settled down into a frozen pose so twisted that Rockson knew the metal man had been wrong.

Chrome could feel pain. And Chrome *could* die.

Chapter 24

The jet sent to rescue Killov came in like a bat out of hell, low over the ice, its landing lights flooding the makeshift airstrip. Killov waved and jumped up and down as the jet bumped down the tarmac and its tires caught, and it reversed power on its two immense ramjet engines.

"Here, I am *here*," Killov screamed, rushing to the plane. Already the cockpit was opening. When he climbed atop the wing, a hand assisted Killov up into the cockpit's second seat. Rockson ran toward the jet, limping, struggling for every breath. But Killov's rescue jet let out a fifty-foot blue exhaust flame and took off nearly straight up.

Rockson fell to his knees, his head lowered. Defeat. After all this, defeat. The fifth missile was headed toward Century City, and Killov had escaped.

Hopeless.

But wait! Rock heard another screaming noise in the blackness above. A second jet came roaring down the runway. It was a jet similar to the one that had picked up Killov.

Inside the second jet, Lieutenant Minhoff hit the brakes. He was confused. Was it *he* that was supposed to land and rescue Commander Killov, or was it Dersky? He wasn't sure, so he had made the decision to land, reasoning that if he was wrong, he could always take off again, and if *his* plane was supposed to pick up Killov, he'd better do it. It was the wrong decision.

Rockson didn't know what the hell this second jet was about, but it was not the time to look a gift jet in the intake. *"Here,* comrade," Rockson yelled in his best Russian, pouring on the leg motion to reach the jet. He was already on the wing as the pilot turned his flashlight on him. "Commander, I—wait, you're not—"

"Dustevedanya," Rockson snarled, hammering the pilot in the face, and pulling him out of his seat. He ripped the helmet and dangling oxy mask from the man's face and threw him off the wing with a powerful heave. Rockson donned the helmet and assumed the still-warm leather seat. He manually pulled the cockpit glass closed and snapped the seals.

But now what? What the hell kind of jet was this? How the hell did it work?

He frantically looked about the Russian-labeled buttons, switches, and dials of the control panel. He felt the stick. He had studied Soviet planes; the Freefighters had most of the blueprints back in

Century City, the result of a vast network of spies who had infiltrated Soviet fortresses throughout the United States.

Rock's near-photographic memory struggled to figure out which instrumentation he was facing. In a flash he realized he was staring at the control panel of an Ilkin-33 trainer jet. *Of course*—that's why it had two seats, one for the novice pilot.

Trainer jets were easier to fly, and they had computers to take over and correct deadly mistakes. Sometimes voice-activated computers. If only he could turn it on. Or even find the damned thing. There were two red switches, labeled one and two, over to the left. A precious minute had already gone by. He had to do something. Muttering "Here goes nothing," Rockson hit the two switches.

The computer said "Activated flight sequence, automatic," in clear Russian, spoken by a female.

Rock sighed. There was a chance—he had flown a computer-assisted jet once before. The details of the control panel, most of which had no identification on its mass of switches and meters, came to him. But his heart sank as he realized something. This was an older model Mach 3 Soviet training jet. It was a "jump-jet." Not built for immense speed, but for short takeoffs and landings. The Doomsday Warrior found the ignition switch to the far right. He flicked it and instantly the engine whined. He trimmed the flaps, and pushing the stick forward, he began taxiing back down the runway. He hit the "biff" switch. It was the control that swung the cantilevered engine to an almost-downward position, for added boost. He felt the huge mass tremble under his seat and lock into position. He shot forward gathering speed on the short runway, hit the afterburner switch, sending a huge flame of blue out behind the jet. The jump-jet shuddered aloft.

"Instructions?" asked the computer. Rock was about to say, "Intercept jet on radar," for the blip of Killov's jet had appeared on the screen. But Rock saw a bigger, higher blip appear on the circular screen. *The missile*, heading south. The thing was an atmosphere-eating cruise missile. If it were a ballistic missile it would be too far away to chase. But it was an air-eater, just like the jet, only unmanned.

Rockson shouted out in very broken Russian, "Plot and commence intercept course on missile, radar screen Vector Eight.

The jet rose through the overcast clouds, the acceleration pinning Rock to the seat.

"Fire all weapons when missile is in range," Rock grunted, his face distorted, his tongue heavy, from the velocity increase.

"Confirmed," the computer intoned.

Rockson asked the computer for time-to-intercept and estimated time of range acceptable for air-to-air destruct sequence.

"One hour four minutes," replied the computer.

My God, Rock thought, this jet *can* catch the missile. But over what area of North America?

The acceleration reached maximum and the jet leveled off at eight thousand feet.

"What location will the air-to-air destruct take place?" Rock asked breathlessly.

A brief pause, then the computer spoke, "Latitude forty-five degrees twelve minutes, longitude one hundred seventy-five degrees twenty minutes west."

"Project map of area," Rock said. A second screen lit, and a map, named and numbered in Russian, showed a blinking red dot in south Oregon. My God, he'd intercept the missile over Dennison City, a Freefighter town of twenty thousand souls. The antimatter explosion would destroy Dennison.

"Computer," Rock asked, "can we intercept missile fifty miles further north, over the high mountains?"

A pause. "Only by lightening our load."

"Explain. What can be dumped?"

"Only weapons are available for dump."

Great, Rock thought, just great! But then he had an idea. "Computer, do we have to drop *all* weapons to increase speed to intercept missile fifty miles north of intercept point projects?"

"Will calculate. Please wait."

According to Scheransky, the missile warhead would make a five-mile crater, and its blast effect would be felt forty-five miles from the explosion. Rock had to destroy it far over the barren mountains north of Dennison somehow.

"Calculated," said the computer, "all but one air-to-air missile must be dropped now to enable craft to intercept missile at new designation."

"Drop all but one air-to-air weapon," Rock ordered. He felt a thud. The plane seemed to gain some speed. The red dot showing intercept location started slowly crawling north on the projected map. Rock wanted to put some more space between the explosion and Dennison.

"Can we get more speed to intercept the missile?"

241

he asked.

"Not possible at this altitude."

"Then change altitude to obtain maximum possible speed," Rock ordered without hesitating.

The jet dove with heart-stopping suddenness. In seconds they were through the clouds and screaming straight at the ground. He fully expected to crash, yelling, "Pull up, pull up!"

The jet leveled off. Rock couldn't believe it—they were about twenty feet off the frozen tundra moving at 2876 kilometers per hour, according to the gauge.

He tried to calm his pounding heart and gasped, "Show new intercept point." The screen showed the red dot intercept-location point creeping north to eighty miles north of Dennison. Barren high plateaus. There was never a happier man. But Rock's smile changed to a frown. Something unpleasant had just crossed his mind. "Computer, how close do I have to be to fire the air-to-air missile at target?"

Instantly the mechanical female voice answered, "Twenty miles."

Twenty miles! But the blast effect was fifty miles wide! He would have to die, in order for Century City to live. Well, so be it, he thought grimly. "Continue on course," he said. "Fire when in range."

He let himself relax in the seat, a relaxation born of the knowledge that he was as good as dead. At least it would be just him. His mind seized on rambling regrets: Simple things, like the fact that he'd never get to give Rona and Kim their neon-rabbit fur robes. But maybe the Rock team would take them back and hand them to the women, and say Rock had bought it for them. Sort of a last gift, a last memory.

Outside the cockpit, buttes and mesa rock were going by on all sides like blades of a fan. The jet maneuvered automatically to the left or right with incredible timing to avoid them, like a steel needle through a garment of solid rock. He glanced at the clock ticking off his life-seconds. Eleven minutes to intercept.

Major Mernik was staring at the Oregon Air Defense radar screens. He had been in the subterranean Monolith war room ever since Killov—who'd been thought dead—had called on air-to-ground radio from above Canada. Mernik had been dragged out of the bathtub and given Killov's order.

"Rockson is heading into Oregon airspace, pursuing a cruise missile. He must be stopped. Scramble all interceptors, prepare anti-air missiles. Shoot any aircraft entering your airspace down!"

But Rockson should have been here by now. Where was he? Mernik wished he knew more about this cruise missile Killov talked of. What was its target? If it was coming close enough to the base to appear on this screen, wasn't *he*, Mernik, personally in danger? Yet as much as he feared the missile, he feared Killov more. He lit another cigarette and stared at the sweep hand of the radar screen. *There!* There was the cruise missile, moving at great speed. Heading due south. The minute Rockson appeared on the screen, the interceptors, which could go 4500 kilometers per hour—twice as fast as most jets—would be scrambled into the air. The six fighters were stocked with air-to-air missiles. They had excellent pilots. Killov's orders would be carried out.

Another blip appeared at the edge of the screen. He waited for it to reappear—but it didn't. What the *hell* . . . He called to the technician at the controls. "What happened to blip two?"

"It's flying incredibly low, Major. Too low for the screen to pick it up sometimes. It's on approximately the same course as that missile, eight minutes behind it.

Mernik yelled, "Call the interceptor squadron, get them airborne. Tell them to fly high, find the jet, and dive down and finish it off. How low *is* he flying?"

"Twelve to fourteen meters off the ground, sir. Much less in spots . . ."

"Incredible. The terrain out there is rocky, there are canyons, hills; the man is mad."

The major rushed to the elevator, took it to the surface—a gut-wrenching twenty-second ride. He staggered out onto the desert surface. He heard the whoosh of the six interceptor jets as they roared off. Russia's best pilots, armed for bear. Six against one. Speed twice that of the Doomsday Warrior's jet.

Would they be *enough?* If Mernik failed . . . his lips went dry. He couldn't fail—he wouldn't fail.

He called his personal chopper pilot over from where he stood at the black-painted command chopper. "Dersh, prepare a flight plan into the east, to the nearest Zhabnov-controlled fortress."

"But—"

"*Do* it. If this intercept fails, neither you nor I wish to face Killov's wrath, is that not right?"

The man paused for a second, then snapped out, "Yessir!"

Chapter 25

Six Soviet interceptors appeared on Rockson's screen. They were above and behind him, and gaining fast. The classification flashed on the screen next to each blip. MIG–89, SPEED 4500 KM/HR. Damn—that was twice as fast as he was going. They would be on him in seconds. Rockson pulled the stick back and rose straight up.

Rockson had only one thing on his mind now—destroying the deadly missile. But to do so, he had to survive the dogfight that was about to commence. And to do that he needed to be above them, not below them. He pulled on the stick and the jet shot upward at a seventy-degree angle.

He felt . . . so tired, every bone in his body aching from the accelerations and the pressure changes the plane had put him through, from the tension of flying between ground obstacles, from the torturous fight with Chrome. But he had to control the pain, control it. . . .

The six interceptors were now twenty-three miles

away! It was beyond the time for thought, it was time for gambling!

He pointed the jet directly at the blinding white sun above. *The Sun. The Lamp of God.* It showed the way! He pulled the stick even further back, and as he rose sharply upward banked the jet directly at the sun. The pursuing jets, although they didn't need visual sighting to fire their air-to-air missiles, needed a radar lock on him.

Rock would give their air-to-air missiles a choice of *two* heat sources now. One was the engine of his jump-jet. The other was the greatest heat, light, and radar source in the solar system—the sun.

He was twelve miles up when six yellow blips left the six blips behind him. They had all fired their missiles! Six Stingers with heat-homing devices. He'd be blown to smithereens if any one of them detonated near the aircraft.

But the burning sun misled them. The six Soviet missiles came screaming by Rockson's jet bent on destruction. They roared up toward the stratosphere. They would expend their fuel long before they were even ten miles further. They'd never reach their hot target 92,000,000 miles away.

Rockson, smiling in relief, banked the jet into a long rolling dive perpendicular to the radar indications of the six jets, which were breaking formation. Rockson couldn't hope to match the six interceptors in speed or firepower—or even pilot skill. But the trainer jet he was in had one small advantage—it could "biff." Most short-takeoff-and-landing jets could do it. To "biff" meant that Rockson could slow his airspeed by putting the engine on a *tilt*, as he had positioned it at takeoff. As a result of the engine tilt, the forward speed was reduced to subsonic, and then could rapidly drop to *zero*. A pursuing jet, without the "biff" capability, would zoom past—and present its butt to Rockson's short-range guns.

"Biff, baby, biff," Rock yelled, hitting the takeoff-position switch on the engine. He felt the dizzying sensation of coming to a near full stop in midair. The nearest interceptor jet zipped past on his port wing. Its startled pilot, expecting this to be more of a turkey shoot than a dogfight, twisted his head around to near breaking point. His target had vectored at an impossible forty-five-degree angle and dropped behind. He began a long curve and drop to come around. Too late. The machine-gun bullets fired by Rockson's jump-jet came right up his tailpipe, blowing the Red interceptor and its twenty-million-rubles worth of armaments and engine to hell.

Rockson tilted the engine back and sped away in an accelerating upward curve. Another Red jet got on his tail. Rockson almost sickened himself with a series of barnstorming stunts—rolls, biffs, and dives—that none of the five interceptors left could match. Soon they were scattered among the clouds for a hundred miles. And since they had no visual sighting, and their radar at ranges greater than five miles couldn't tell an interceptor from a jump-jet like Rockson's, their eager pilots locked onto the closest targets, let fly air-to-air missiles at one another. Two blips fell from Rock's screen.

Each pilot, seeing the air-to-airs approaching, bailed out, their ejection seats catapulting them into the sky right over an area Rockson remembered was the domain of the Bright-Face Sioux, a particularly warlike tribe that liked to bake any Russians they found on stakes. So much for them. Three to go!

But they were piloted by men who weren't so foolish.

Rockson watched the three remaining interceptors on his radar, slid his jump-jet into a swift descent, and dove into a narrow canyon. Hopefully they'd have a tough time picking him up on the radar with all the metallic rocks around.

"Where the fuck is he, Deskenov?" snarled the pilot in the lead interceptor as the three MIGs swept right by the area Rockson's jet had vanished into.

"He's down there somewhere among all the damned rocks," the second jet's pilot replied. "We'll soon get a heat trace of him."

"Fire in bursts, at random, all along the canyon down there—he's likely to get hit."

"How will we know if we hit him? We can't tell Killov we *think* we've killed the Doomsday Warrior!"

"Fool, there will be an explosion. Stones don't explode! We will know if we hit him. Now lay down a field of fire up the canyon to the west. I'll fly along the east arm and do the same. Volik, you follow me a minute later."

The jets dove, roared level about seventy feet off the rolling terrain, letting loose bursts of cannon fire and an air-to-air missile from time to time. Rockson saw one coming, veered right. He winced as the missile passed him and destroyed a huge chimney of red sand to his port side. A few rounds of cannon fire whizzed past his cockpit and chipped holes into the splendor racing by. But they were shooting blind, Rockson's jet's exhaust heat often hidden behind towering pillars of sandstone. He zigzagged between two buttes, almost clipping one.

Rockson saw his chance and he took it. He biffed the jump-jet once more, and he saw the startled expression on the MIG pilot who for the briefest of instants saw his jet when he slid by Rockson. The Doomsday Warrior fired the last of his machine-gun bullets after the Red jet, managing to catch the port wing-flap. It tore off the wing-flap, which bounced down among the canyon rocks. Unable to steer, the Soviet pilot had a good view of a particularly brightly striated mesa, dotted with sagebrush, glowing in the pink winter sunset—before he died.

Rock biffed to a stop and set down his jet on a sandy beachlike area, where the roaring creek in the canyon made a gentle turn. The jump-jet's wheels grated and grinded over the gritty sand and came to a bumpy halt. Rockson let out a sigh of relief and cut the engine. He hoped that this desperate trick would work. It better. He was a sitting duck now.

The first and third MIG pilots saw the explosion of their air buddy's plane in the canyon. And their computers fooled them. The Soviet interceptors' computers found no trace of the exhaust heat of any aircraft below and therefore reported, "Target destroyed."

The two remaining Soviet pilots sighed in relief.

Their comrade had made the supreme sacrifice. His jet had, no doubt, run into the Doomsday Warrior's jet. They peeled away, climbing high, then took a vector back toward base to report their victory.

Rockson watched them disappear on his radar. His joy was shortlived. He was alive, but the Megon-II missile was still heading for Century City. He had lost precious minutes—perhaps too many! He hit the starter, heard the engine turn and whine up to takeoff power. He tilted the big engine for an almost-totally-vertical takeoff and hit the afterburner switch. He rose quickly out of the canyon on a tower of blue flame, and then he angled off to the south, narrowly missing the lip of the canyon as he gained speed and altitude, back on the chase.

Seven minutes. The whole air battle had only taken seven minutes. But that meant the damned hell-missile was seven minutes closer to destroying all that Rockson lived for.

The computer informed him that the missile he was chasing had diverted west to circumvent flying through a megastorm of winds over 380 kilometers per hour.

"If this jet goes straight through the storm," Rock said, "can we make up seven minutes of flight time and intercept missile at last point projected?"

The computer said, "Yes. But tolerance of this jet is exceeded by winds in storm ahead."

"Proceed shortest way to target."

"Proceeding."

Chapter 26

Rockson saw the flashing lightning. A brewing blue-black thunderhead appeared directly in front of his jet. He knew the storms with the blue-black clouds packed tornados. This could tear the plane apart like a matchstick.

The Doomsday Warrior plunged his jet into the hellish turbulence nevertheless. Immediately the plane began yawing violently from side to side. He trimmed the flaps and the craft steadied. Lightning bolts yards wide crashed by to his right and left. He watched the radar. The missile was there, off to the west. He flew onward, into the sodden clouds that buffeted and rocked the little jet like it was a fly caught up in a giant's hand. Blue crackling "ball lightning" attached to his little craft, crept up the wing, and flashed itself out.

The lights went out in the jet's cramped cabin, the instrument panel went dead. The lightning had shorted everything, Rock realized.

As the plane began to nose over he found the

auxiliary power switch, clicked it, and some of the panel including the radar lit again. But the altimeter was spinning off his descent. Why? He was encased in silence. The engine had flamed out! He was falling out of control. Altitude 25,000, 20, 15, 10 . . . and a downdraft was making his descent more rapid. *"Restart,"* he yelled. No answer. Computer down too! Where was the fucking restart? He hit every switch he could find. Bursts of de-icing fluid exuded from his wings. Martial music came on. His seat moved back. Finally he heard a whine. He had found the restart. The engine was turning over. Five thousand, four thousand, and still dropping.

Suddenly the jet's engine roared to life and he pulled the stick violently toward him. At five hundred feet he began to rise again through the drenching rain and wind.

With a sweaty grip he returned the jet to course. And the storm raged on, buffeting winds tearing at the jet. Where was he? The computer light blinked on. "Computer, project our position."

He was still somewhere over Oregon. There on the radar screen was Mount Hood. And the blip that was the missile. Twenty-one miles away! A sudden windshear threatened to smash the jet down, more lightning streaked across the sky, one jagged arm of white death touched the port wing and tore off several heat-tiles. Rockson fought with the stick; the plane was like a leaf in an autumn squall, rocking, plummeting, and then—amazingly—the storm ended as quickly as it had begun. Rockson hit the afterburners, which should only have been used for takeoff. It increased his speed, but it wouldn't last. It was gobbling up his last fuel too. The computer said, *"Pilot warning A."*

At a speed that was heating the wingtips white hot, he tore across the now-flat sagebrush-dotted prairie, sending up a sandstorm of dust in his wake, shattering the ears of a thousand gophers and chittabugs, creating avalanches from the echoing concussion of his passage in the nearby hills. A race against the total destruction of free man, a race to save the world from the clutches of the drug-crazed Colonel Killov. One man, with one air-to-air missile, one desperate man with but one last chance to save humanity.

"Emergency abort," warned the computer. *"Speed too great for structural integrity of plane. Automatically slowing airspeed."*

"Override, override," Rockson screamed. *"Manual speed control."*

"Negative," said the droll tones of the computer. *"Slowing to mach two."*

Rock's heart sank. What could he do against the computer? *Right! Pull the plug!*

He took out his knife and pried the panel off the computer console; as it fell to the floor he cut the red wires inside the panel. The computer started saying something, then stopped. Forever. The plane started to gyrate wildly. Rockson took the stick and increased altitude. He leveled off at 6500 feet, keeping his eyes peeled ahead and the stick tightly in both hands. Still possible to catch it—with all the acceleration power into the engines. The plane's wingtips glowed white; heat began seeping into the cockpit. The plane was about to disintegrate. He

253

looked at the radar screen. Range dropped to twenty and one-half miles. *Almost there.*

Suddenly he saw the missile visually. It was passing over some jagged peak—elevation fourteen thousand feet—a mountain! Maybe there was a chance he could live after all! The Megon missile's image on the screen started blinking. IN RANGE OF TARGET printed itself out on the radar screen. Rock hit the firing switch for the last air-to-air missile and watched it shoot forward in a blaze of smoke. Immediately he eased down on the airspeed. He twisted the stick, and a second later dropped the jet behind the giant granite face of a high peak. There was a too-brilliant-to-watch flash beyond the summit. The air-to-air had destroyed the Megon.

Rockson was still alive. The immense peaks had shielded him from the full force of the antimatter explosion.

Rock landed in a steep canyon, this time smashing the plane's wheels to a torn, useless junkheap under the jet. The plane settled in at a crazy angle in the sand and gravel, having gouged out a long skid mark. The nose bent over. There was smoke. He hit the cockpit release, and the canopy shot away a hundred yards and floated off in some rapids.

Rockson jumped out of the steaming jet and ran for what looked like an indentation in the canyon wall to his left—shelter of some sort. It was fifty feet—and he dove headfirst into the little cave. The concussion of the antimatter explosion, some twenty miles northwest, rolled down the canyon walls loosening boulders, nearly bursting his eardrums.

He pressed to the floor of the shallow cave until the

rolling thunder of rocks and falling boulders subsided. Minutes later, Rock crawled out of the cave and looked around. The jet was in no danger of flying again. It was so twisted up that Rock surmised a boulder had rolled over it and continued on. It looked like a fly squashed by a flyswatter. But it had served its purpose.

He started walking down the canyon. Walking toward Century City. It was hundreds of miles south. But he had some daylight left. And tonight would be clear. The stars above would guide him. He was alive. And Century City survived. But what of his men in the far north? Would they make it back? They were resourceful and brave men. They'd make it back—*somehow*.

He coughed up some blood, and with a silent prayer, he began putting one foot in front of the other. So weary, so far to go . . . so very far.

THE SURVIVALIST SERIES
by Jerry Ahern